# HEY JACK!

# BOOKS BY BARRY HANNAH

# HEY JACK!

## Barry Hannah

E. P. DUTTON · SEYMOUR LAWRENCE
NEW YORK

*Published in the United States by E. P. Dutton/Seymour Lawrence,
a division of NAL Penguin Inc.,
2 Park Avenue, New York, N.Y. 10016.*

*Published simultaneously in Canada
by Fitzhenry and Whiteside Limited, Toronto.*

Library of Congress Cataloging-in-Publication Data
Hannah, Barry.
*Hey Jack!*
I. Title.
PS3558.A476H4      1987      813'.54      87-5426
ISBN: 0-525-24558-8

W

*Designed by Michele Aldin*

*1 3 5 7 9 10 8 6 4 2*

*First Edition*

*Grateful acknowledgment is made to the following publications in
which sections of this book first appeared in slightly different form:*
Harper's *(June 1986) and* Southern *(November 1986).*

*Grateful acknowledgment is given for permission to quote excerpts
from* The Korean War: Pusan to Chosin, an Oral History *by
Donald Knox. Copyright © 1985 by Donald Knox. Reprinted by
permission of Harcourt Brace Jovanovich, Inc.*

*For Susan Varas Hannah, my wife*

# HEY JACK!

I go back to Korea. Do I ever. Sometimes I stand on a corner with a book in my overcoat looking up at the sky and begging it to snow. I stand there in my undefended face, no weapons on me, knowing so much it is an agony not to write it down, and thus I have gone home, over and over, and written this down, so as to distinguish my life, which has been not so much lately, and to share the tales of our little town. In that way the sands of time will perhaps not cover us up.

You will find me changing voices as I slip into the—let us say—*mode* of the closer participant. Otherwise I am sane, except for once in my life, and do not speak in tongues or hear voices as they do in certain churches. My eyes get bigger than ever over the situation of this town and my passing through it. I have settled here because of the university library and the distinguished bookstore, and also the old gentlemen who sit on the chairs around the square to reminisce. These old men have not been treated well in other fictions by the authors in other states in other times. But you cannot ignore their wisdom and you cannot ignore the fact that it takes a certain strength to sit out in such a hot shade in the summers and watch the cars and young scoundrels.

We have famous people from here.

"Pa. Is it really true the old eat their young?"

Gives pause.

"Couldn't rightly say, son. I'm a mid man. Feels like I'm walking on ice meself. Go on down to the barn, ask Gramps."

Gramps is down there in the back shadows, some loose bales around his old brogies. Seems to be humming and eating, pulling a nail out of a rotten piece of board with a pair of pliers.

"Is it true, Gramps?"

"Wyoming's not my home . . ."

"Yer nuts, Gramps."

Sings, "Ate ol' granny in a choo-choo car!"

Kid goes back to the hut to see Gramps's father. Withered beyond longevity, a tiny man in dwarf's overalls, deeply addicted to codeine and Valium; fears colored people; occasionally makes scratching protests on his old violin, which has become too large for him. Every disease has had its success with him. Now he's barely a scab demanding infrequent nutrients. Bald as a beige croquet ball, he rolls his own.

They've fixed him up a mike with a cord into an ancient Silvertone amplifying box. Even his snores can be heard, slightly, out in the yard.

"Double Gramps, is it true that the old eat their young?"

"God damn, I'm old!" blasts over the kid, feedback piercing too. The old man faints, recovers, goes into a codeine wither.

"But my question. Please, Double Gramps."

Almost accidentally, the old man fits bow to fiddle and scrawls out the grand trio of "Stars and Stripes Forever." Endlessly. It goes on the entire afternoon, amplifier picking up a prouder stroke here and there, screeching.

The kid grows up, a rock star, ageing at twenty-three. He's already eating the young by the thousands when the second thought hits him.

I knew him. I saw him on the television. His people still live, unchanged except for the mansion he has bought them. I sometimes pity them. They don't know quite what to do with the big house, don't know what to do with each other any more. Being dumb and nuts was their profession, and they could never adapt to any other.

Once there was, here where I live, a tall, pale, hypochondriachal professor whose life and hopes had been so entirely discredited that he slept most of the day, unwilling to expend another chance on life, art, love, or even weather. Yet he would rise occasionally for a purchase on that footage of perfect laziness that amazed and confounded his friends and students and brought with it the inkling of some minor treachery against those who might have been brave or bought, with their little allowances, even a tenth of their dreams.

Yes, never mind that he had height, indiligence, and nihilism, nothing finally came of it except the tired, infinitely tired loneliness that shook from his brows as we watched him leaning somewhere in a hall.

Could he get any paler or any worse? We wondered.

Yes, he could.

One day he set his books and records on fire while they and he were still in the house, this house he had purchased and which nobody had visited much except for select protégés— always handsome little men with tucked-in underlips. Even these little men did not know what to make of his despair. Was it despair, even? They doubted sometimes that he was energetic enough for despair. Rather, he enjoyed very much, it seemed, the despair of others.

He stayed in the smoke and the flame until it was unbearable.

Then he went outside and sat in his car. The smoke had made him want to urinate. So he got out of his car, though he had half wanted to drive somewhere; but where was he to go, with all his friends, those dead book writers and composers, smoking in there?

When he was taking a leak behind his car, his own car (some unfortunate toying with the gearshift lever), it rolled backwards on his greatly steep drive, wildly in neutral, and rose over him, knocking his head to the pavement. Thereupon, his head exploded in horrible pale matter.

# HEY JACK!

Hey Jack? Really really horrible.

I call to Jack, who sits with the old fellows around the courthouse, those ancient mariners in this landlocked and soily town, where the big oaks sway and the giant magnolias stand huge and firm, ready to make themselves near naked when the cold weather comes on.

What shall we say, also, of the other dead one, our dentist friend, Jack? So privy to him we were, and yet he died something of a secret.

He was out in the country with his dog when he died—"broke but happy," he told my father, who is a very old man now, with a patience that is practically exasperating. The dentist left us guessing, and yet I with my arrogant hindsight may supply this for him:

The old man hears something at the window.

He has been out here a good length of time now, all alone and wishing for nothing. He brought a book with him, but he has not read into it yet. He was out at the old homeplace, where his mother and father raised him. Out here, he could not remember what the book was or why he had wanted that particular one.

There was a dog with him, but here the dog was, lying just under his nose. So it was neither the book nor the dog making a noise at the window.

When the old man was fierier and younger, he had had politics. This was just after the demise of Senator Joe McCarthy, but he had clung to the beliefs of McCarthy, had our dentist friend, telling his patients that it was a difficult time to work in, very difficult, what with a Communist occupying the White House. The patient could not reply to him because that metal draining hook was exhausting the blood and dental matter from her mouth (this woman would marry and have children and then become my lover) at the time.

The dentist was not used to being replied to. A dentist may go through life without any true conversation at all. That perhaps is why so many dentists are strange, lonely, and depressed men, so many of them committing suicide, with the easy access to nitrous oxide they have. If they know nothing else, they know that nitrous oxide is good stuff. He had never thought of doing himself in, even after he found out that McCarthy had been called bogus. Yet he had often thought of doing some of the *world* in.

He had bought a copy of the *Manifesto* by Karl Marx. He began reading but found it totally incomprehensible. In college he had read *Mein Kampf* straight through, with pleasured sighs, then slapped it down with the triumph one sometimes has of reading a completely satisfying novel at the beach. There were the stains of tears around his eyes, because he had drunk a pint of bourbon during the last half of Hitler's book, and there was something sweetly joyful and sinful in reading it late at night, his roommate snoring stupidly away on the cot across the room. The bourbon was secretly joyful and sinful too, because this was a religious college that enforced the rule against drink on the premises very forcefully. No matter, he never forgot the delirious thrill of that book, though he had been a dentist in the army and done his part against Adolf. At the end of the war, however, when everybody knew the Germans were in rout, he recalled how sad it was to reckon with our white men killing their white men, and a great regret came over him, especially with the Russian Matter looming up almost instantly.

With some of his money in his fifties, in fact with a large part of it, he invested in a combination swine and potato farm. This was the upshot: All his help quit one day, leaving for Detroit, and these men, these three men, deliberately left the gates of the hogpen open—during a hard dry season—and the hogs ate the potatoes. They ate them so much that most of them died.

He could not reconcile himself with such spite.

He put no stock in psychotherapy at all. Look at the lone psychologists in town—a married couple, the Beeflows. They gave their only son, whom they had not wanted especially and called openly to his face "our drunken accident," everything that came into a teenager's mind: motorcycles, a Volvo coupe with two carburetors, high fidelity records as soon as they appeared in the stores, five-dollar haircuts. The mother was a chain-smoker with a practically murderous glare from her eyes for the locals. She and her husband were from, and educated in, Chicago. Our dentist friend could think of nothing worse than entrusting the life of his mind to this woman.

He went seven counties and 150 miles away to seek counseling. He went to Meridian, trying to understand the spite of those black men who had thus treated him. He went to a real psychiatrist, a man with an M.D.

Still, the drive down was nervous. What if anybody ever found *out*? What if his *wife* found out? She was a nurse, and very good-looking, though sometimes leaning toward the portly. She had large warm brown eyes, and their children were beautiful mainly because she was beautiful. He almost never saw his boys, and the boys were effeminate. When he was in college, a smart-aleck friend of his roommate's had called him "epicene." He had stood there and taken it and, when the fellow left, had looked up the word and was horrified.

The psychiatrist worked above a shoe store. His own offices were much better than the psychiatrist's, who was very young, wearing thick glasses, bright red hair on his head. He was having a bad time himself, in Meridian, and about this he expatiated. His receptionist had just quit because he'd cut her off Valium.

They were meeting at straight-up two in the afternoon, and this was a significant time, almost an oddly magical time, said the young psychiatrist. You must remember, he told the dentist, psychiatry is new to Mississippi. It came in about the same time as TV, say '52 to '53, and was met with much greater hesitation than "Hopalong Cassidy" and "Our Miss Brooks." Now, since it was 1959, but only 1959, there was still resistance. People were ashamed to speak of their troubles, the trouble in their minds and with their fellows, and about their lack of sleep, their night sweats. They might be just a little different from those around, just a little, that's all, and still they were ashamed to confess that difference, especially in this state where a man was raised to barely ever confess even his physical ailments.

"I'm not ashamed," the dentist lied.

I can see you're a different sort, yourself, the young psychiatrist went on. The dentist wondered if he'd looked that young when he first did his citizen practice. The man was so young, one ray of sun could come across his face and reveal him as a veritable (how our friend, the dentist, loved that word, using it five to ten times a day) *boy* from a tenth-grade class. His accent was Southern. Maybe he was *from* Meridian. But his language was animated and brilliant, and very soothing. The dentist wanted to ask where the man had gone to school, but he decided this would be unmanly. He would look at the certificate on the wall when he left.

So what, proceeded the psychiatrist, Dr. McRae, is on your mind?

"The niggers that were so mean to me."

"How's it going with the wife? I mean frankly the wife in bed, doctor."

"I didn't drive all the way down here to talk about Sigmund Freud. I'm paying cash. I had this hog and potato farm—"

"How did you feel about the . . . 'niggers'?"

The dentist didn't understand what he wanted.

"Were you cruel to them in any way, do you think?" The young man lit an Oasis cigarette. "Did you pay them well? What is your attitude toward Negroes in relation to yourself?"

"I was never cruel to anybody in my life. I paid them twice what they were worth."

"What do you mean by that?"

"Twenty dollars a day."

"For all of them, all three?"

"For each one."

"I've never heard of a white man paying that much for farm help."

"Ten dollars a day, then. But also gasoline. God damn it. Also I got them free service at the emergency room."

"For what?"

"For cutting themselves up after they drank. Good Lord, man. Where have you been? Then, I bought them cigarettes and food."

"You ever take a drink with them?"

"No."

"Does your wife treat your body like it was magic or does she just shut her eyes and give you the usual thing?"

The dentist refused to answer.

"Are you a 'nigger-lover' or a 'nigger-hater'? Which one, would you say?"

"Middle of the road." He looked around the pathetic dusty office, with only the one certificate on the wall. It smelled of cigarette smoke, and he could smell food from a discarded white bag in the wastebasket. Dr. McRae was still sitting on his desk in the outer room. Weren't they supposed to go back and get on a couch? There was a working air conditioner in there, anyway, and it would be a much better place to be healed in. There was also some nice soft furniture in there. He must have been looking at it wistfully.

"Sure. We can go in there if you like."

He went in and the psychiatrist shut the door.

"In this state, doctor, I find there are exactly five subjects: money, Negroes, women, religion, and Elvis Presley. The rest are nothing," said Dr. McRae. "Strip off, how about it?"

"What?"

"Take your clothes . . . like off."

He never went back to Meridian.

He knew young Dr. McRae was not nuts or queer. The psychiatrist was moving him ahead very rapidly toward an understanding, and he knew it, and it was just too frightening, the pace. He had understood that years were entailed in this therapy, and that one often became friends with the psychiatrist. This young man did not really seem to care whether the two of them were friends or enemies. He was working toward something very quickly that was so clean, pure and radiant and true, that he did not want to see it (our dentist friend) and still did not.

Was it the memory of the young psychiatrist knocking at the window when he went to bed?

Now he was sixty-six years old and he wondered if that young man was still in the state, or even still alive, still as clear, radiant, and moral as he was almost thirty years ago.

During the years, he was kinder to blacks, and yet he could not help being terribly interested in the Atlanta child murders. The man they had arrested had spoken of the numbers of blacks that could come from one young black male, and how if you could just destroy one, you would take hundreds away from the earth. Our dentist did not want to kill anybody personally, but he thought of the idea, very profoundly, of how perfect it would be simply for there to be fewer people around who never paid their bills and had no two thoughts about it.

The schools integrated.

His wife left him, for the older doctor that she had been a nurse for all these years. He had barely any money left. Had the blacks who owed him money for their teeth ever showed up and paid him at once, he would have another fortune.

His sons were off somewhere, ignoring him. He was not even certain what work they did now. It was all right that he was a "failure"; that was all right. He would live out here at the old family place. He described himself to the few acquaintances around town as "broke but happy"—the few who bothered to ask or even recognized him any more at the village grocery store, which an Indian couple had bought.

The town had grown very much. There were some tax advantages and good schools for white people who worked in the nearby city, and the town was spread out in subdivisions around the old little village with brick streets, the college, the great Baptist church. Some of the homes south of town were worth upwards of $300,000, he'd heard. He didn't know. What was sure was that the old town was grown and gone, and there was nowhere else to escape to.

He had run from the young psychiatrist in the fifties, the young man who held truth like a candle as in one of those old Fisk ads ("Time to Retire"), the lad with the tire around his shoulders—the heaviness of the truth of a good tire, the candle blazing in total darkness, and the little boy in his sleeping gown, waking up beautiful and cherished in his innocent be-seeching expression.

Oh, he wasn't going to run away from this place, even if the colored people showed up and paid him everything suddenly. The town was almost around him, anyway. It had nearly sprawled out to the old homeplace itself.

Here he was left with his dog, an amiable long-haired cur with the great warm brown eyes of his wife, and the growing lawn in the pines and the kudzu creeping on their trunks. Nothing ever showed in the hot drenching wet sunlight of Mississippi beyond a few cats looking for rats and little rabbits outside.

He was out here on the remnants of the very farm where he had had the swine and potatoes, and his meals—such as he could choke down—were mainly canned meat, crackers, and the tomatoes that came from the ragged patch at the backdoor steps.

Still, he could swear he heard a noise, a definite noise, at the window where the air conditioner was working. It happened at night only, never during the day. Because at night there came a tapping noise. He could not find a flashlight in the house, not one that worked. The others were frozen up with their oxides. There was a definite tapping, such a definite tapping that it woke him off his perch on the chair in which he was sleeping.

This time he was readier. Last time he was at the village store, he'd smiled smally at the smiling incomprehensible Indian behind the checkout counter. It was a new Ray-O-Lite flashlight, utterly trustworthy, he knew by damn, a thing in the night like that child with a candle, its eyes wondering, with the tire of truth on its shoulder.

For three weeks he's heard this tapping, tapping, tapping at night.

He was in his old bent-down tennis shoes, but he raced in them around the house, not even waiting to be scared. Certainly, by damn, he wouldn't linger any more about this issue. He knew he wasn't crazy, he knew he wasn't. He had never been crazy.

He wanted to prove this.

At the air conditioner outside he saw a tall man he took for a teenager, a yellow-brown young man, tapping at his window. The young man froze and looked on as straight at the light in his hand as he could.

"Who are you?" our dentist friend demanded.

"I'm Dagen Sayers," said the young man. He now looked to be about twenty-five.

"Sayers. Like Dagen Sayers that worked for me here. That let my pigs—"

"His son."

"Why. What—"

"Daddy's dead. But I come back to mess with you."

"Mess with . . . but *mess*?" he asked.

"Confuse you, white man. Mister Dentist. Con*fuse* you."

Our man was gone then.

So was his heart.

It would be nice to say the young man knew him and brought him into the emergency room, but it didn't go that way. He made a call to one of his white neighbors, a man nouveau riche, and depthless in his understanding, and horrible to his mind.

And this is how our dentist friend went away, already dead but leaving a handsome, lean, gray-haired corpse behind.

His hair was risen up in waves, like an evangelist's.

I tongue the delicious (somehow) open space of my absent tooth behind the molar where the dentist jerked it, for being rotten and unsavable. It is back there and not unsightly, though through the years my teeth have leaned out of their normal positions to compensate for it. Such it is, I often think, with the deaths of others we have known slightly. No more, no less, and somehow slightly delicious after all.

Jack is a better man than I. He never needs a drink and barely even smokes. He wears ageless clean clothes, always impeccable in their used way. Buttons the top button of his shirts regardless of the season. I suppose he found this style in some comfortable season of the past and never changed it. He is nut-brown but fairly unseamed, for all his days in the sun. He had cattle and soybeans in years past, neither failed nor succeeded with them, but had enough to buy the coffee shop near the railroad, where the college kids come and some of us older folk too. I was fifty before I considered myself older than anything. As for Jack's age, he must be twenty years older than I, but there is a pleasant accord between himself and the passing times that almost belies age altogether. He will take a drink, mind you. You will recall I mentioned he never needed one, and there is the vast difference. You can bring your own liquor into the coffee shop. He neither encourages nor resents it. But you can detect a little sadness in his eyes behind the wireless spectacles when somebody gets obviously lushed.

Jack knows the rock star, knew the professor and the dentist. All of them have been in the shop. The hard thing is, though, nobody really knows Jack. They know his slight smile. He is something of a slimmer and less gaudy Teddy Roosevelt, with his twinkling glasses, the trim athletic build. An old tennis player, one would guess, one who went all the way back to the really old wooden relics of rackets, women playing in bloomers. But he has never been an urgent historian of his own past, not even when he accepts the rare straight shot of rye from the hundred or so I have offered him. He belts the shot in two swallows, then takes the Lucky Strike from my pack and chases the burn away. Soon he will look merrier (no watering of the eyes or coughing), but there shall be no moisturizing about ancient days. Jack is no gabby philosopher. He has been a man of action, and now he is quite at peace as a shopkeeper, always polite but never groveling, as you find in the false little country restaurants hereabouts. ("Hi, y'all! Come back, honey!") Christ, the South has been pickled in the juice of its own image.

I asked him once if he was hiding a gunshot wound with his collar buttoned that way.

He smiled as if beholding a massive impertinence, then lowered his eyes to the cup of iced Dr Pepper that he favored in the mornings.

"I meant, because you were a sheriff once, in Kentucky," I said.

"Not a dumb gunslinger, either," he said. "Sheriffs are overrated anyhow."

"You ever get horny?"

"I was so hungry and horny in Paris once, I began crying while walking over a bridge."

Crying?

"Were you going to jump off the bridge, Jack?"

"No. I'd written a poem I thought was immortal and I didn't want to get it wet. I had it in my pocket."

"So obviously you went and found a woman." Then I joked. "A woman with a loaf of bread under her arm."

"Well, at the *exact* time, I just threw the poem in the water."

Jack has been married three times. He is a fine-looking man and all his wives were handsome. He never says a bad word about them and sometimes sees his last wife in Arkansas. They go up to a cabin together, near Mountain Home, where they cook with wood and fish for crappie at night with a lantern, the cold mists of the Ozarks falling off the mountains onto the deep lake around them. Jack once took me there. We had fresh crappie out of a heavy skillet and I remember to this day their succulence, cooked with butter and pepper. The moon sits on the lake and you can hear the rough little sounds of large birds flying in the night. Also those loons crying, or whatever they are. Maybe the rednecks have shot them all by now.

Jack indicated to me once that two of his wives were quite alive and all the divorces had been easy, in a way, because they had the mutuality of his daughters, one with each wife. He never lost contact with his daughters. They all had a college education and were only four years apart in age.

The only thing he hated, Jack said, was that the rock star, now thirty-three, was seeing his youngest daughter, who was forty. With all of rockdom and its harlotry to ask for, he was seeing Jack's pride, Alice, the schoolteacher.

The fellow was dumb as a post, Jack said. His manager had never allowed him to utter one single phrase in print. He had never been interviewed, only photographed. Jack had threatened to kill him. Outside of this matter, I had never seen Jack much upset.

"I know there must be some charm in how he sings," he said. "Then his looks, lean and hungry. One could pity him for his dead fathers. But all of his folks have been dead since they were born, though they go on living."

Jack had taught criminal science at a small college in Maryland once. He knew a bit about the mind of them, he said, and he suspected the rock star had it. Look how he had treated the dead professor's daughter.

"The jackass had to come *home* for his romance. Had to revisit the scene of the original crime of his conception," he said.

Harmon thinks he is a dude. Harmon is nothing. He is not squat. I hardly think of him at all.
Nobody thinks of him. He has hardly occurred
to their brain yet. In his neutral-tone shoes and
shirt with spiders on it and belt with leather
smiles on it, he is Southern trash and would be
Northern trash if he was up there. He walks like
somebody's supposed to be looking. There's
Harmon, wants to be known as *Harm.* I have
expended study on him. Nobody gathers my
hatred into a space like Harmon.

Harmon comes down the way in his sev-
enth car of the year, some leaking jet-wing
flyer that he thinks is a racer, through the light
that he sees. He is a high school graduate just
barely, and he's got his sunglasses on. Harmon believes he is something. He is tall and
handsome. He thinks he is a free power. He
doesn't have the guts to enlist in the service.
He'd rather stay around town and burn gasoline, being a delivery boy at a grease palace.
His father had died and Harmon's mother had
made Harmon dress in his father's army suit
and read his father's love letters to her. Somebody had tried to get Harmon to enroll at the

college, but Harmon was too smart for the college. Watch out, watch out, for Harmon. He is a large chickenshit who likes to beat women. He likes to wallow around in mud in a pickup truck.

I was talking about Harmon with some of the fellows around the courthouse. Harmon himself had just cruised by, and we were saying that people like young Harmon would better serve each other by going back up in the hills and committing incest man on man. Or having saw fights. As it is, the riffraff is on the increase, mufflers leaking in your air and annoying your ears. Can't hold a job, can't hold much but their own dick.

I saw them in Korea, all sorry soldiers. They couldn't wait to get back home where the *real* wreckage was.

I saw Harmon come in Jack's shop once. Wanted to know if Jack made onion rings. Jack said no, but it was more how he looked, like very neither did he make room for the likes of him. Then I knew: If Harmon had any talent he could be the rock star himself. And Jack knew that.

To make things short, I am in love and I am also a veteran of Korea, with the big guns pointing straight at me, never knowing when and if they would announce: You die. You die, man in green, with three quarters of your college education and all your memorable thoughts about the threat of snow in the air (still love the feel of that humid threat, heavy with meaning), all that behind you now. All of that over, because the snow will snow on your head dead as your love for the wife back home, and no children. Not even a poem or decent letter left behind.

But now I am in love with a woman I met at Jack's café. The world is so small. She knew the dentist, as I have said. For some reason followed his career and unearthed it for me. Although she was forty-one, her hair was charging blond from her head, and her gray eyes were full of happy light.

Suffice it to say about my profession that it requires only half a day of intense boredom and then I am free to commit trouble—or find vision, on the lucky days.

My hair is white, but I still have all of it. I am fifty-six. I keep a fairly lean body. They used to call me Sabre Jet in my late twenties. I'd appear on the tennis courts and could run any ball down. "There's Sabre Jet," they'd say. Women were there, around, all right, and I was divorced and knew I *should* be in love with two or three of them, but I simply wasn't. There were some delectable choices among them, and they treated me deliciously, but I was shy of love. I suspected it ended at orgasm, for the main reason that my own affection never went further. I was not such a hard man as a suspicious man, and I had in me that fugitive poet's soul, not so long ago released from the gunsights of the NKs. I wanted to breathe, and I wanted to breathe my own air, my own Lucky Strikes, the fumes of the rye whiskey I had so elegantly adopted in an officer's tent in Chosin once I knew it existed; to breathe, also and best of all, the smell of new books and old books, gamey with life and thought. You open some fine old books and smell Russia itself.

I had a whiff of one one afternoon that was exactly the aroma of Chosin. How could it be? Then I went nuts. But for only a month.

Enough about me.

Jack Lipsey attended the professor's funeral. He felt something sad and resonant. Perhaps we were both shocked that the man had died in such a colorful way, seemingly beyond his energies. Something about the hideous comedy had made his corpse available to a lot of us. There were many people at the funeral, held on an airless hot afternoon in August, an antipathic day for such a pale and air-conditioned man.

The professor's daughter was there, of course. She was a brunette of much poise and beauty. I like to see patent leather heels on fine tanned legs. She was stunned but graceful. No weeping from her, only a look of concerned terror, so that the purse in her hands was trembling.

Behind her I was extremely surprised to see Ronnie Foot, the rock star. At first I didn't recognize him for his black funeral suit and white shirt, Ivy League tie. There was not a thing flashy about him except for his long black hair, which was glistening in a gorgeous way under the bald sun. I noticed he wore a vest and had a small pooch to his stomach. Otherwise the man was lean, white, and, except for the penetrating stupidity in his eyes, could have passed for a lengthened choirboy. My eyes went beyond him to the black limousine and the man with a driver's cap held to his heart leaning against it.

When the service was over, I tried deliberately not to look at him any more, and I offered my condolences to the daughter, as did Jack, who invited me to ride back to his shop in his clean old Buick. I usually walk, and I hardly knew Jack then, but it was such a distinguished offer, when I looked at him, I could not refuse. And I must admit the air-conditioning in the old Buick felt good.

"You like to walk, don't you?" Jack said.

"It's about my only exercise nowadays."

"You don't care for cars?"

"I have a Renault at home."

"And you're a bachelor, like me."

"How did you know?"

"The look. Besides, you told somebody that in my shop the other day."

"You don't seem to be the kind of man who listens, the way you put your foot up and stare."

"I think a man who doesn't listen is a fool. What do you think I want, your money?"

I said nothing; neither did he for a while. I thought it curious that a café owner didn't want your money.

"Do you drink?" he asked.

"Four drinks a day, every day," I said.

"Do you have any at your house this Sunday afternoon? Terribly hot Sunday."

"I've got rye. That's what I drink."

"Could I have a glass?"

"Of course."

"Do you play golf? Would you like a game later in the week?"

"No. I'm no golfer."

"What are you?"

I mentioned my profession. He seemed satisfied. You always wanted to satisfy Jack Lipsey.

We got the rye and went to his shop, which is no distance from my house. He had been interested in my old Renault. He popped his lips slightly and walked around it with a keen eye through the sparkling rimless glasses.

Now that we were at his café, he took out a shot glass and I filled it. He took a Lucky Strike from my pack and downed the shot in two gulps, then quickly lit the cigarette. I wondered how many shots he would want, but that was it. Something was on his mind. He seemed to know something all of a sudden.

"He was there for her," said Jack. "He had the look of the wolf about him. I can tell you where he is right now. And she's with him."

I looked at him. I'd been planning to get high, then have some of his cheesecake.

"I was a bohemian." He pointed to his own chest, then pointed his finger out at the world. "He's simply a destroyer. He destroys hotel rooms and he destroys little girls. When he gets forty he'll change, settle down, mutter something about finding himself. But I don't intend to allow him that privilege."

I didn't quite know what was wrong, but I held my counsel, seeing the fury in Jack's eyes.

"You fought for freedom in Korea. And

myself at Normandy. Later with Patton. This is not freedom. He's come back to the county. Everything that America can buy was not good enough for him. He's come back to destroy his own people, and the best of them. A rooster, a chickenshit Sherman, turned back on his own."

I thought he was drunk off the one shot and envied him.

But then we got in his car and drove back toward the cemetery. The limousine was still there, alone and imperative, with its darkened windows. The driver was standing out in the cedars, rubbing his head with a handkerchief, cap in hand. The windows were smoked glass, I think they call it. Jack knocked at the rear window, then yanked the door open.

"Hey, man!"

She was giving him a blow job with her skirt over her lovely rear raised up so he could get a finger in her bottom, but now he was climbing out of it.

"Get away," said Jack.

"Cecil, get me out of here!" Ronnie Foot yelled.

The driver started running. He got in the driver's seat, slammed the doors, and you could hear the electric locks go down. They pulled out, going around the turn and back out to the street where her little economy car sat parked, light-blue and humble. The limo humped the curb right by it and damned near hit it.

"In her grief," said Jack, and then again, "In her grief. Before she had another mind."

"She's a big girl, Jack," I said.

"Did you smell the lavender cologne coming off the seats of that car?"

"Yeah."

"Nobody's that big. The cologne and the Big Time. No woman in grief is that big."

"Why does it matter so much to you?"

"I have daughters. You ever have a daughter?"

"I have no children."

"Have them. Then talk to me."

She came by the shop two weeks later. I wasn't there, but Jack explained.

"He used her and threw her out. She's nothing but living shame. She's a wreck. She had to take two pills while she was here."

"Why did she come here?"

"I knew her father. He was just a poor tired hermitsexual."

"What?"

"I said a hermitsexual."

"Oh. What did she want from you?"

"Some kind words."

"And what do you want from her, Jack?"

The question interested him. He put down the checked towel he uses on the counter and the tables. Pushed his glasses up on the bridge of his nose.

"I want her to be safe and free."

"Like when you opened the car door on them?"

"You'd think she wouldn't appreciate that for a long time. But she already does."

"For her own good, or yours, Jack? Did you operate this way when you were a sheriff? Yank open private doors?"

"No, in fact I didn't. That was a broad job. This one is narrow."

"Did you appreciate her ass with the garter belt and everything?"

"I did. I'm not a dead man."

"Just checking."

"I didn't think he would get to her that fast."

Mama and Daddy round up each other and come in, sit down in front of the video screen, all kinds of video tapes scattered around the VCR. Daddy farts and says "Uh-oh!" Mama laughs. "You're a sketch."

Tonight they've decided they will have just some mashed potatoes with Mama's special heavy greasy gravy. While them 'taters is makin', they gone watch some young Ronnie on the box. They live in a mansion Ronnie bought. It was built fast and is already turning into doodoo, things falling out of the ceiling, black widows and brown recluses having a field day all over the corners. At night the roaches come in and heave off huge crumbs, which are everywhere. Ronnie comes on the big screen. They play him without sound, and then Dad starts banging away on Mama, who is a big woman.

It's ecstasy out at the Foot mansion. They don't use the top floor for anything but Gramps and Double Gramps, who won't die. Gramps likes to get tight on Stolichnaya and shoot his .22 at the chickens outside. He also has two open-ended mailboxes mounted in one window, and he will bring two or three chickens up, put them in the boxes, and push them out with a plumber's friend, to see how far they can fly. Some of them have been pushed out so much they are wounded and fall straight head first to the ground like a chicken rocket out of fuel.

Gramps is not allowed to carry cash, but he awards the chicken winners dominoes of high points, which he tapes around their necks. That makes them skinny too, because of the hardship of eating or drinking. Then he shoots them and eats them. Every winner loses.

Double Gramps never awakens. He is in a coma of sleep, but in the room there is a four-thousand-dollar stereo playing constant fiddle music and ocean noises.

Mama and Daddy's ready to eat them 'taters now.

He smacks the ball, a crisp shot to the green. Puts the iron back in the golf cart. Then we go across this footbridge, looking over the hill for the green. When we get up there, there is no ball. I'm enjoying this stroll but I don't understand where the ball could be either. We look around and there is still no ball. I walk by the flag and happen to look down.

"You holed it, Jack."

He strides over to the flag with that almost prissy military gait he has, his shirt buttoned up to the neck. Now it's fall and nippy. He gets his shirts from London.

He looks down at the ball in the hole.

"I've never done that in my life."

Then he bends down to pick the ball out.

Straightaway the crack of a small rifle comes out of the swamp next to us. I hear the shot skim off some bark, and the next thing I see is Jack's bloody hand holding the golf ball.

The bullet passed through the web of flesh between his index finger and thumb. He'd put his other hand over the broken vessel. It didn't hurt, he said. He was still holding the golf ball.

I looked through the trees and there it was, the Foot mansion. They'd come to town.

"You all right? I'm going to talk to the bastards," I said.

"I'm quite all right. Don't do anything."

"Why not? The bastards."

"It was an accident. A ricochet."

Jack smiled bigger than I'd ever seen him smile. He looked entirely satisfied.

Then almost it's too good together. There is no time except time to waste, between my lover and me. She will go through the house naked or, better, half naked, the more appealing to me personally. It is true I had something to bring to this place myself. I have been preparing to be a lover for thirty years. Now all my nights are anointed with oil. Now the smiles and the laughs almost never cease. It is ridiculous how much you laugh when you are in love. You seem to have ridden time down, the wild stupid violent horse, and brought him down between you, so that he lies there exhausted for a long, long while. Her bare feet are together at the end of the bed. Your underwear feels good on you, also the water from the shower, with your face revealed, naked and with no weapons. All the great words of Keats, Shelley, and Shakespeare are whistling in the air, coming in the cracks in the windows and down through the holes in the roof. Some of the music piles up on the bed, and you can practically kick it off the sheets.

"You so sweet to me," she says.

"That's my occupation," I say.

She has a nice deep California voice, somewhere from north California.

"You're good with words," she says.

You bet. I'm such a clever bastard I should be in some ad for romance and Lucky Strikes.

"And you're handsome," she says.

"My God, girl. Gimme some love."

The threat of snow was there, and then down it came. We went out on her porch to watch the streaks it made against the streetlights. There is a suddenness to snow in the South, such a beloved reprieve from the usual, when the hot houses just stare at each other and the neighbors come out to knock on their lawns with implements and vacant eyes.

The dentist's son sat in Jack's shop, sipping his freshly squeezed orange juice, with coffee on the side. My woman and I were there, being in love and assured of our arriving marriage in the spring, in a far booth at the back. Maybe we were having bagels and cream cheese, onions and pepper on it. Jack cuts up the spring onions, the bagels are always nice and warm. We sat there trying not to observe the dentist's son too openly. He was a solemn fellow with a receding hairline, sitting there in the uniform of the bread truck that sold bagels, rye bread, onion rolls, and pumpernickel to Jack. It came out of Memphis. The man had strong arms and a big belly. You would figure that he ate a good fraction of what he sold. He had begun as handsome but now he was swollen.

"He's a sculptor," she whispered.

"He is? What kind of work?"

"Found art. Kinetic things in wood and metal. Old airplane parts and cypress stumps, things like that. You'd like him. He's not a bad man at all. A little bit pitiful and lost, but he's married. I hope whoever she is helps him."

She used to work in the art department at the college.

He nodded familiarly at her and then came over. He had on those grim black utility shoes. Already I felt sorry for him and liked him. His greeting and his smile were shy.

"How's it?" she said.

"Sometimes it flows. Other times not. 'Bout with you?"

She introduced me. There was a good spirit in his eyes. You could believe he was a good baseball player who had let himself go for a long summer. He said he's seen me walking around town.

"I'm not too interested in sculpting any more," he said. He took a seat on the edge of the next booth, then faced us. "Went to the Memphis Academy of Art. I'm cashing it all in. I can't care that much about it any more."

"What's wrong?" she asked.

"I drive around and see all the wonderful junk lying out there. I want all of it. What this country has left behind is three whole other countries."

"It sure is. Thinking about it, at least."

"Well, it drove me near crazy, what people throw away. I couldn't organize anything any more. I couldn't make any more connections. *Everything* became a connection. Let me tell you, when everything is a connection, you better quit the game."

"I would think you, as the artist, would

make only your own personal connections," I put in.

"Have you seen the junk in the world lately? 'God didn't make no junk.' You've heard that saying. But man *did*! Man *did*!"

He was getting loud and Jack looked over.

"You get in that bread truck between here and Memphis and see the junk! The junk! The junk! We've got to get cleaners in here, selective cleaners. We can't go on looking at so much junk. Mechanical and human junk. Junk! I tell you! Junk on TV, newspapers, left and right. Church junk. I'm going back, I'm going back, I'm going back up in there, up there deep, not even taking my wife. I'm giving all that up. Giving it all away. She doesn't talk anything but old female junk anyway! I'm getting out of here!"

Jack looked over at the table. He didn't comment on the volume of the fellow's voice. I was about to say something, but she put her hand on mine. I was stirring. I have never got used to being yelled at. This man was going on like a chubby Hitler.

"It's maybe not best to leave your wife," she said.

"Thanks for your nice advice, but I guess I know when, God damn it, when to leave. Not to ignore you. But you don't know yet. Only *I* know! Only *I* am the authority!"

"This could be said in a milder voice," I said, taking up for her, being her protector.

"I'll show you *mild*!"

"Hey, sir," said Jack, calling him down.

The man left the café.

He did not look back at his bread truck, and he was gone from the vicinity.

We sat there, she and I, loving away and trying to make a laugh out of it, but there really was no merriment here. Jack looked downcast and studious, with his neat London-by-way-of-Hong-Kong shirt buttoned up to the jugular and his healthy ashen hair swept back neat, parted on the left like a trench.

There was a long silence all around the little café.

"That family has had trouble for a long time," she said. She had her gaze still at the window, pathos in her gray eyes. Her legs were next to mine. You don't think too much about the agony of other men when you have such active and helpful legs near you. The season was Christmas, almost Christmas.

The rains had come in, and Jack was fairly bored when he couldn't get out on the links a couple of times a week. But the coffee in the machine smelled good, and her neck was full of perfume. There were good warm winter smells loafing around the place.

In the winter we played some poker, at

which Jack was an ace. She played good poker too. Jack liked her around. She tickled him, he said. She had great tenderness toward Jack, because it was here in his café we met, and here I was, fifty-six, in love, and hoisting around the trophy of this blond forty-one-year-old lady.

Here was Jack, seventy-seven, once a war correspondent, once a sheriff in Kentucky, once a college professor of criminal science in Maryland, once a busted soybean and cattle man in Mississippi, now an owner of Jack's Café, come back to sit down and spy at the town just as I was. Jack spoke German and French.

I am perhaps handsome, with my white hair, but all of it still on my head. I, after Korea and the lucrative jobs in between, and my going nuts for a month when I smelled that book that smelled exactly like Chosin, but otherwise sane—all these thirty years I was preparing to be a lover.

"Just a minute. He's back," said Jack. He was looking out into the small rain, and there was the dentist's son with something in his hand. "I'll be. He's slashing the tires on the truck."

We stood up and the portly fellow was jabbing a knife into the front tire. He knew what he was doing.

The truck began sinking as he walked around it. It took him about thirty seconds to do all four tires. The big thing sank down and was wobbling out there in the rain; then something popped and it just gave up and squatted on the rims.

He was gone again after that.

She held on to me and she whispered.

"You won't ever be that nuts, will you?" she whispered.

I was staring at the place where the young man just left in the right window. I really sort of loved him.

"No, honey. Not again. I've already done it," I told her.

Another Marine veteran of Korea lived south of town. I knew nothing about him until I heard about the death threats. His old mother took care of him when he was out of the ward. First I knew of him, I saw a curious large personal in the local paper. He desired a wife. He was *of artistic temperament, suffering from a nervous disorder. Desire a wife who will be confidante and friend.* There was an address and a phone number. It was a pathetic cry from one of those mournful country houses on the highway you see between towns. You could smell terror as sharp as garlic off this ad, and you could smell the odorless Thorazine too. *Veteran of Korea*—the pride and the horror at the same time. I had no woman then, yet I felt everything that he felt, almost, in my loneliness and my "artistic temperament." Three Chinese field armies crossed the Yalu in October 1950. They were volunteering like mad across China, wanting to kill us. Kill us in the rocks and in the pine trees, at a mean temperature of minus four degrees. We were in their back yard and they wanted to kill us very badly and there's little else to it, as that awful schoolmaster history tells us, that bald, dull, correct old-man history. We had beaten the NKs, we'd pulled down the Stalin posters in their capitol. We had the Corsairs, the Sabre Jets, the F-80s, the napalm, and the white phosphorus. But it was their winter, not ours, and they had the bodies and the poverty and the Russians buying the tickets and cheering. We were Custer all over again at Chosin Reservoir. About five times I would not shoot out my whole clip on the carbine. I wanted at least two shots left. One for the gook nearest me when the horde came on, and the other for my brain.

"Desire a wife who will be confidante and friend." It sounded like the burp guns, and it smelled like the garlic and the frozen rocks and that cold hard steely smell of somebody else's snow. It sounded like the air liaison officer in the rut next to you pleading for the Corsairs to come back and do the same thing again. It sounded like your own arty tearing up the mined field thirty yards ahead of you.

Then I met her and she told me, "He makes death threats over the phone."

"To whom?"

"To anybody who gets any attention in art."

"What should he care?"

"He went to school here in the art department. He did some kind of painting and everybody thought it was bad. They wouldn't give him a private show. All the students got a private show, but they thought his stuff was so bad it would embarrass the department."

"You ever seen any of it?"

"No. That's been a long time ago. He's called Bob and Dan. He called that professor whose own car killed him."

Bob and Dan were painters, very good ones. I'd always envied both of them. They took me through their studios. Bob was the fastidious one, always working on extra textures of real things. Dan was less the draftsman. He considered life a large violent sexual circus and his paintings were huge, came at you like cartoons splashed across tents at a state fair freak show. I had begun writing in my notebooks then, and I envied them the way they could have an entire realized picture in an afternoon. I wrote so slowly, my only companions fear and coffee.

"He threatened the professor's life because the professor had written several articles about local artists in which he was not mentioned. The professor purchased an alarm system for his house. He also called up the chairman of the art department, who's a woman. Come to think of it, he never called Bob or Dan personally. He called their wives. He told their wives that he was going to kill their husbands."

"For being artists?"

"For getting a little bit of recognition."

"But I guess he goes on painting? He thinks his own stuff is great."

"Nobody knows what his stuff is any more. He lives with his old mother. Ask the sheriff. He comes home from the mental house down in Jackson, he's fine awhile, and then he gets on the phone. The sheriff goes down there and escorts him back to the mental house. A sad case."

"He never came into town and threatened anybody's life in person?"

"I don't know. I don't think so. I can tell you *like* him, don't you? I'm sitting here, as sexy as I can be, ready to do anything for you, make you any supper you can dream up, and you're more interested in him."

She had the prettiest little feet. Her sex was

narrow like a girl's. I am a big man in muscular shape, despite my Luckies and my rye. You can stay in decent shape when you play tennis three times a week. She was a good scrambler at the game. I'd bought a new modern racket. a new Wilson wood. We'd had some fine points together at the university courts. My serve was coming in so well for me one afternoon, I thought, Well, hell, I'm as good as I was at twenty, when I was a Marine lieutenant and had nothing but my lungs to carry us out of Chosin. I got the Silver Star. A skinny little man, scared to death, got the Silver Star. She was hitting back some of those wonderful serves. Thing about her was that she loved me and would never give up a point unless I blazed a winner. She wanted to stay in the point so long, it was like making love when you never want it to end.

But she was right.

I wanted to know about him. His name was Wally Cooper. I went by Jack's café. Wanted to know if Jack wanted to go with me.

"No. He's a lunatic. You examine that word and it means moon-mad," said Jack. "I've got another kind of mad. Ronnie Foot is with Alice tonight. He's messing with me through my daughter. I mean business. I have my old gun."

"When you were a sheriff, how many guys were shot?" I asked him.

"Three. Me included. Just a twenty two in the hip. I was running away from a lunatic."

"You're beside yourself with anger."

"I've got to watch myself. And I will. I don't need any company or counsel."

In modern life there is no sheriff and no police and we all know it. If you are in jeopardy with your feelings, there is no one at all. The police come around to laugh about the fire. The police in this town hate the citizens. One night the big wooden Warehouse restaurant, a nice mall made of wood, caught on fire. It was two doors down from us. I was in bed with my lover. She went down to watch the fire. The police were laughing, hating the students and the bars in there. People watch "Hill Street Blues" and get the idea that cops are human. This is an interesting theory, but the truth is they are cowardly thugs, armed with shitty little hatreds such as leave them heroes in their dreams. They watch television when they are off duty, are in love with machinery and guns. Here they harass tight citizens and never solve or help in a crime, because of being chicken. They listen to the radio. They are fat, stupid, and officious. Their motto is "Quick to Bust, Slow to Serve." There is an academy of cops here. They are abetted by an ugly stunted judge named Preen.

I cranked my Renault and went down there.

He wasn't home. He's been taken back to the asylum. His mother told me. She was younger than I expected. She was a vigorous old silver-haired lady who didn't want me to go in the house.

"I'm a Korean vet too. Just wanted to see what he was doing. Wanted to meet him."

The hot wind was blowing and he wasn't there. Around the house, a nice planked country home in the shade of two giant pecans and a big oak, you had a hot desolation of old hot time. But the old woman was steady.

"He don't want people seeing his works yet. They're all unfinished."

Everything around the house was brown. We had had a bad drought, and I could see up close now what a hell of a thing it was to be a farmer when this long heat came on and you didn't have anything but the crops. I saw the murdered soybean rows and looked across at the little airstrip where the crop dusters flew, and I saw two of the pilots doing nothing over there.

"I'd like to go in and see his paintings. I really want to, ma'am."

"Well," she said, letting me in the door. "There's a whole lot to see."

I looked around. In the back room the large canvases stood on the floor. I know nothing about art. But it was motion art, kinetic, no pictures, only the nervous soul. All of them were terrible. Given thirteen paint buckets, I could have done them during one of my night-mares.

"He liked a man called Jackson Pollock. He was a beatnik for a while. He read a book called *On the Road.* I liked him when he was a beatnik," she said. "He loved me so much when he was a beatnik. Nothing was wrong."

"Where was he in the Marines? Do you know?"

"He got lost. They shot him up so bad he got lost."

"Where? I'm asking because I was over there. All this life is gravy to me," I said.

"He was crazy before he went. He was an artist. He was my only son and he was a beat-nik."

"Why is he nuts?" I asked her. "It's been a hundred years since Korea."

"He needs a wife. He said he needed a wife in the paper, and none of them came down to meet him."

"He worded himself badly," I told her. "It scares people."

"He can't help it!" she screamed. "He was shot three times at Pusan."

That's all I needed to know. He wasn't just a nut. There is a guy who works the library here, but who more regularly works one bar. He was smart, he was artistic. They drafted him and he was so afraid of getting over there, when I was already over there, that he tried to commit suicide. He was given a medical discharge and has been in care of the Vet Administration from then till now. They give him Ritalin and he drinks wine down at the bar. He's queer and very kind to everybody, totally inefficient at his job, gives out this barking laugh with a maimed curl to it, the exact reveille of the Korean experience, he having never even been there. Rather helplessly, I have affection for him. In another way, I found a kind of mirth and even necessity in Wally Cooper's death threats. Had he called me I'd have been flattered.

We took a trip to Florida, she and I. At the air base near Panama City, on our way back, she insisted we stop. I saw what she was looking at—how could you miss them?—but after the calm of the ocean and the old shabby-genteel house we had been in, with its screened porch running around the vast quarters, the old shell collections, souvenirs from Africa like the crossed spears and shield from brothers who don't die like we do, and the worn proud aromatic books about the sea and far parts (plus the rows of innocent sleazy old detective fables); after the sun and the moonlit walks, the lotions, the comfortable burned skins on us as the breezes rushed through the living room and moved the squeaky swing on the porch; after all that lush prevarication and nightly rolling of Mother Ocean ("It's all right, it's all right; everything is calm; we are just eating every thing that moves in here, dry people"); after being assured that nothing was wrong with anything as long as you just got stupid, peeked out at the lunar water, and thought the stars meant something to you personally; after the revenge of the penis on lost time, the sucking of the vagina so vigorous and miraculous in its greed for every rocking motion and drop of sperm—well, I almost wanted to skip these old relics of jet aircraft they'd posted outside the gates of the air base. They went all the way back to *me*, for God's sake. There was the F-80 and the famous F-86 Sabre Jet. We stopped and got off to walk on the asphalt tour, with the signs describing each jet's history and use. In the blazing June sun, the jets looked flaky and ancient, forlorn and disremembered, despite and because they were flung up at the tourists' eyes. I could have been looking at the very machine that saved my life, but the paint was dry and cracked, the interiors as wizened as the face of Orville Wright.

I was somewhat depressed. She couldn't understand it.

We were going through a glorious pageant of flight, but I just wasn't in the mood. She was very excited about seeing these old vets from Korea. She described them as hardware phantoms of the imagination. Imagine Leonardo da Vinci, she said. I wish he were here right now with us, she said. She was a spunky and gorgeous little blonde who rarefied my entire idea of myself, being seen with her on a hot Florida highway. I felt like a genius with a lot of sperm invested in her. My bouts with ulcer and recent bad teeth, even my morning cough from the Luckies, seemed to have a point. Nothing seemed meaningless junk any more.

I was suddenly proud among the old jets. My depression went away. All the energy of our lovemaking came back to me. The sun was not so oppressive now as it was sparkling and close. I had *fought* for this little piece of museum turf outside Panama City. I was much *older* than these jets. I was older than the sea and I was eating everything in sight. My hair was as white as the sun.

On the way home I had an oyster Po' Boy, a big bag of boiled peanuts, some salt-water taffy. I had two cups of coffee in Hattiesburg and a big Polish hot dog with kraut. When we got home I went to the Jitney Jungle, bought a

carton of Luckies and an enormous jar of pick-
les, dilled in the exquisite dry Jewish way. I sent
a check in to Amnesty International. Bought
some garlic and Vitamin E capsules because of
wanting to live and be handsome forever. Saw
a little mirror somewhere in the grocery store
and swore to get my teeth cleaned. I promised
to go light on the Luckies, maybe just fifteen in
twenty-four hours.

I was back by the milk, just standing there
enjoying my prospects and my first Lucky in an
hour and a half, all alone, returned from
Florida with my tan, looking forward to maybe
just *two* rye whiskeys, when this attractive
woman that I knew came down the aisle, looking tired already, though nothing was in her
cart. She was a tall woman, almost tall as me. At
my age, all the lookers were married or memo-
ries, and she was one of them. I liked her full
lips and her yearning eyes, her bare legs that
looked like they'd run swift on stupid missions
all her life. Back and forth with great earnest-
ness in behalf of nihilism. Rut-born. She was
married to a monster, and I knew him. I'm
going to surrender this poem now, called "A
Guy I Know," her husband:

*Now is the hour.*
*Now is the time.*
*I must get my uniform sewn*

*And repaired by my wife,*
*So I can climb into the machine again*
*And sell needless shit to scared people.*

*Nobody can guess how lousy I feel*
*Inside, how I have to stop at*
*The roadside bars and explain myself,*
*Always telling lies, one after the other.*

*I pretend I'm interested in life and my fellows,*
*Pretend I'm a good husband*
*And complain about all the nasty laws preventing*
*Me from being even worse than I am.*

*Then I sneak back home.*
*Christ, how I hate her,*
*Especially when she submits to me.*
*I am a man, and this is the only way to be.*

He beat her. She was probably having a migraine now, awaiting his arrival. I know these things simply because she told me them straight out once in the doctor's waiting room, she with her migraine, me with my ulcer. An ulcer simply hurts. A migraine is a hell where suicide sounds easy. I once heard a sportscaster say that a tall Negro star with a migraine headache played a basketball game for Los Angeles or somebody. Somebody was a lying motherfucker. Nobody has ever played shit with an active migraine headache. She was one of those women you want, the anguish is coming out of her eyes and who has such superb legs and her children are from a bad man. Such anger brings on a bad poem. It makes you count out one-two-three-four-five-six, and the rest. How can I enter you, let me count the ways.

Etc.

We let these things pass, and it goes to the calm thoughtful zone, that old untroubled spot where nobody is guilty, all is forgiven. All is forgiven. Come home.

Come home, baby.

Come back home, baby.

Come back home, baby, to me or I'll kill you.

There was so much lead in the air at Chosin, and I am so lucky for crawling away from it.

We went up to Little Rock and Nick Butler had an automatic water gun like an Uzi with a water clip, lying next to a book called *Red October*. He put the clip in and the thing shot around the room. It worked perfectly. We were impressed. Actually there was very little to say. There were a lot of important authors in the room, they had written their guts out, and there was nothing really to say. Arkansas looked good, the river running through Little Rock. Dee Brown was there last night. Nick's wife was out trying to sell his books. She was a beautiful woman named Jamie. I was nobody. I was an unpublished author with his blond lady. It was perfect, for me, because I had nothing to say either. Nick had built a new room in his house and we were sitting there, very pleasant. I was drinking coffee and we were talking about odd things dragged up from the bottom of a pond, yes, somebody, all of us were dragging up crawfish from a pond, the man was saying there was a great snapping turtle in the net, talking about eating turtle and the different tastes it had, and I had seen a movie where they boiled fish, the first time I ever heard about somebody boiling fish. I was thinking about Jack, wondered if he knew. Or how he could be that old and never drink too much or if he knew how I was so wanting and she was so willing she stood in her den with the TV running and let me take her with her blond trim ass up, looking like Miss America's ass, and I had my will.

One day I saw a Chinese Communist young man so willing to die, with his white fur suit on, I shot him to pieces before he stopped smiling. That's when I knew we needed out of there. All the bullets in my carbine were gone. Everything from me was gone. I was cold. I wanted so badly to go back to the hot South, with the girls around the tennis court. That's where I went.

Alice, his darling, was threatened. She was of age, she was of plenty of age, and he only happened to know about it, but now that he did, he knew too much history and he was near insane. The history that you know is fine and dead and clean, all in order. But when it comes near you, even if you are a previous sheriff in Kentucky, running the county full of wild men and whiskey makers and their daughters, when it is Alice, your daughter, you don't get any previous dead run of events, and you do not care especially for the language of history, as old as you are.

Jack was completely new, in his hate. He was a man I had seen before but never in this version.

He was taking out his pistol and showing it behind the counter. It was a long-barreled .38. The big slugs looked golden to me. I never considered the beauty of these heavy loads under a lamp, though I guess I must have jammed in hundreds of them in clips when I was a young man over there. Jack was unhinged. I talked him back. I counseled him. His eyes were bright and he was sorely depressed. He kept handing the gun from this hand to that, he stood up suddenly, he sat down, deflated by his audaciousness, having served somebody coffee with the weapon in the other hand.

Ronnie Foot, the rock star, had her. Or Jack thought he had her, he was sure he had her. Jack was mumbling. Jack was talking about ingratitude and pride and scum hanging on meat, things of that nature. It was astonishing to see him creep and rise suddenly, like a crazy old man.

He was just standing there looking out toward the window and thought he saw Foot's limousine flash by under the streetlights in the rain, and he thought he saw his daughter Alice, the schoolteacher, next to him. He turned toward me and said, "They're flaunting me. Flaunting me. She looked like just a ghost of my daughter, flaunting me."

By then I was with him for morning coffee. His old, speckled right hand, with the scar from Grandfather Foot's ricochet red in the fingers, his glasses down on his nose; the way he ambled instead of really walking in his old erect, slightly military way; mentioning also that he was taking more cigarettes from me and, being never a beggar, finally bought a pack of Luckies for himself; the good man looking straight down at the floor for minutes and minutes—I was alarmed but also glad, because he had joined the region of *me,* with my flaws and my littlenesses.

"She was either not there at all or what you saw, I don't think she was flaunting, by what you've said about her." At this time I let go this terrific fart, held in by wisdom and ethics for twelve minutes. Nobody else was in the café, and the thing rang out for almost a third of a minute, no smell accompanying, since it was all mostly mental.

Jack put his glasses back up.

"Nobody ever had a daughter like me. You want me to just let her go, like a fart?" He was fingering the gun again.

"Talk it over with her."

"She won't talk to me about it. She's in love."

In love, in love, in love. A mule can climb a tree if it's in love. A man like me can look himself in the mirror and say, I'm all right, everything is beloved, I'm no stranger to anywhere any more. I'm a man full of life and a lot of time to kill, shoot every minute down with a straight blast of his eye across the bountiful landscape, from the minnow to the Alps. Something looks back at you with an eye of insane approval. Something looks back at you; out of belligerent ignorance of you it has come to a delighted focus on you and your love, together, sending up gasses of collision that make a rainbow over the poor masses who are changing a tire on the side of the road on a hot Saturday afternoon, feeling like niggers. There is a law that every nigger spends a quarter of every weekend changing tires, my friend George, the biochemist, says. What do we know? What do mere earthlings, unpublished and heaving out farts like wonderful puzzled sighs, know, but what is in our blood? I had broken up once with a woman who was in Europe, and coming out of the mall movie (I don't even remember the movie) I gave out this private marvelous fart that was equal to a paragraph of Henry James, so churned were my guts and so lingering. And I was free. Free to discuss it. Delighted in the boundless ignorance and destruction that lay out there under the dumb lit cold moon.

Enough about me and my poetry.

Lexington, Kentucky. He was a sheriff from a well-tamed beautiful rolling county in southern middle Kentucky. He had won $5,600 from the Derby races, using a tip from Peter Rice, the sheriff in a county that bordered Ohio. There was a little sheriffs' convention in 1953 in Kentucky, and Jack had recently stood up to receive an award for best lawman in the state. An enraged and drunken team had rushed him with knives out. He'd shot them both in the leg, backed up, taking a knife wound in the shoulder. The newspaper report acclaimed his bravery and noted that he had no hard feelings and would press no charges until the two of them were out of the hospital and sober.

He was still weak from his wound and also from the publicity given him. But he had an eye for poker and won nearly $10,000 from the white people too drunk and rich to really look at their cards. The money, big bills piling up on his side, and Jack putting them all in his breast pockets, made him look like a big muscular man. He had bought a nice white tweed jacket with blue threads running next to the white. When the lights were turned off and he went out in the dark to his car, he looked like a Hollywood swell. He looked like a big swaggering millionaire, a "dumb bull's-eye," he said. He'd had only two whiskeys, but the money made his head swim, along with the memory of the award, and he was almost blind with self-esteem when he reached his car, a new and shiny Mercury. Two thugs out of the dark came directly on him. He was stabbed again, but they couldn't get through the money. He was simply knocked out by the rush and awoke in the front seat of his car with his slim self and thirty dollars, exactly the cost of driving back home, and the big rich empty coat. He had had it with cities. He'd had it with being a sheriff. With awards. With everything that made you notice-able, everything that made you the dumb bull's-eye.

He tendered his resignation. They refused it. He tendered it again, in stronger terms. In that he was gone, to raise cattle and some cotton if he could find it; maybe even rice. Just something, back in the poorest state of all, Mississippi. He had a notion that he could be rich unto himself if he went down to the worst rectangle of geography where there was no hope at all, so that he could build himself into a strong man again, piece by piece, no thugs jumping on him, just mosquitoes and his old age. He had married a woman who was a Kentucky aristocrat. She was beautiful and wanted to make love all the time and other-wise was a bore and a nag. A woman who wanted up so bad her head overdrove the rocket and wound up in the mental home of a horrible county in South Carolina, where she killed herself just frankly by putting a tiny hid-den .22 hollow-point bullet in a hidden Satur-day night gun into her mouth and pointing it north, *blang*.

I urged him: Jack, Jack. Get a hold. Take some time off. Get drunk on my bottle of rye. Lie down, lie down in your old bachelorhood. Alice is only your daughter, maybe an accident from a great love forty years old, not a child. Nobody can really pull that much wool over her eyes, not Ronnie Foot. You don't think he could have any real claim on her, do you? And so there is a little vacation into fame for her, so what?

"I believe I'll have my own feelings, thank you," he said.

"Without the thirty-eight, I hope."

"I *mean* the thirty-eight, but I'll find another way."

"Good for that."

"Her mother killed herself, and I'll be damned if she will too."

"Oh. I'm sorry. I didn't connect."

"Consider it connected," he said.

In the afternoons I look over the town. Nobody hates reality on a sunny day in the town more than I do. I have despised reality since youth. I will do anything to spoil the functioning money-taking reality of a good stupid summer day in this town. The Civil War was not started by Harriet Beecher Stowe, as Lincoln said, or Sir Walter Scott, as Mark Twain said, or by economics, as somebody said. It was started by about a thousand towns like this, bored out of their minds.

Yet I take money and have five nice-looking suits and speak low and slow and literate. That's what I do in the mornings.

In the afternoons and at night I look over the town.

I lose myself in the stories of our friends in the town. I go out and stand around in their stories. Don't get too close to me, husbands, wives, and lovers. Nothing is sacred, I tell everything.

We came back from a county trip, Jack and I, and in the headlights we saw this beautiful nourished coyote male swerve and dart back to a pasture. His eyes were bright and he was blond, healthy, and running. Much smarter than your cat or dog. The people who used to ride for the foxes with their teams of dogs are now running the coyotes in north Mississippi. But coyotes are smart; they can leave a county between themselves and the hunters, and when they turn on the dogs they can fight. Among horse people who hunt, the coyote is hardly ever even *seen*. He is a scent two miles away before you hear the hounds and kick your horse. They say there are one hundred thousand of them in the state now. They've come back to Mississippi from Texas and the West.

I fall asleep at night thinking how wonderful it is to be surrounded by these thousands of brilliant coyotes: a whole new beautiful nation around me, barely even glimpsed.

One time I went back in the pines of Neshoba County. I expected the worst things at this gathering around the old house, which was burned to the soil. My wife's grandfather had died by going back to his house where his money was under a mattress and he wanted to get it out, though the house was burning. He was a lovely man, generous to his children, though he had nothing to give. We had all gathered there, on a hill in the pines of Neshoba County. The county was ugly from the road, all red dirt and pines. I got disattached immediately. I had an attitude. I was smarter than these Neshoba County people, back in the sticks and the pines.

Then Uncle Bill talked to me, in his straight clear country talk. He liked me, for some reason. He was eighty years old. He was listening for the sound of the panther down in the swamps. Then he would let his dogs loose. We were out under the chilly moon near his dog pen when I heard that shrill hoolering crying thing down in the swamps. Uncle Bill, with his lantern and his gun, stood up higher, and I can believe his ears rose in pleasure, to look at his smile. It was a Mississippi bobcat he was listening to, though the country folks called it a panther. It sounded like a dying woman, verging into the pitch of a banshee. Uncle Bill let the dogs go.

"They love it so much," he said.

"Well, are you going down after it?" I asked him.

"No. My brother just died. And you're my guest."

"But you got your lantern and your gun."

"But you're my guest. You've come a longish way," Uncle Bill said.

I was suckling my Luckies like crazy out at the chilly dog pen, under the raw white moon. His brother had just died—been burned up and buried—and he liked *me,* out of all the people in his long bulging cabin of a house, with dog manure and cold doom in my nostrils.

Then the coffee was made. They poured it straight into the water and boiled it. This coffee, poured out through a sieve and drunk with milk and sugar, worked on me like diamond speed. I had real Dexedrine when I went back to college and memorized entire books of chemistry and algebra, but this was better, out in the sticks under a ten o'clock moon with Uncle Bill, who was ready to go down in the swamps, but he liked me. His brother had burned up four days ago but he was ready for the panther or me, and I was doubled over with hospitality. I even loved my wife.

I loved the panther down there, and hearing the dogs after it was a direct kind of music that woke up my dull ears and my dull head.

"What do they do if they tree it without you?" I asked Uncle Bill.

He gave a long smile, taking the twelve-gauge shell out of the broken shotgun.

"They have fun arguing. Then they come back home."

I was looking at him, admiring his eighty years. He was in his black funeral suit and a starched white shirt with an orange-and-purple tie.

He smiled.

"The panther likes it too," he said. "It's been years. I bet the scoundrel's big as a calf by now."

Now that old man is dead too. His brilliance flares out in my head like the flare of my Zippo lighter as I get another Lucky. I have the great advantage. My universe is growing smaller. No-body has a prayer if it's getting any bigger. Thinking of infinite largeness is what drives people nuts, I say. I stand uncorrected. All you need is a roof, a prayer, and some pussy.

Mister Sermon out in the snow with no weapons except his right hand with the pencil.

Which says Jack was in a panic, though he had promised me that he was calmer.

Little Alice, forty, once married but no children. She teaches Spanish and history to tenth-through twelfth-graders. She has had no lover for more than three years, and she re-minds me of me, who waited so long for something good. Her husband was not a lout. He was simply a banker in Tupelo who bored her. He was a decorated vet of Vietnam, but he was one of those who got back *too* sane. Like a good Southerner, he clung to his mother, an ageing alcoholic with legs like yard chairs and a belly like a watermelon full of acid. Alice felt denied and insulted. She didn't care for him physically that much anyway. He began getting fat and he was hairy. He was swelling and he paid no attention to much of anything but philosophy, which proved that everything was futile. He stayed at the library, reading science fiction. He had begun as a handsome decent man, and now he was swelling into a hairy-cheeked milky-looking face with an effeminate drawl. All of Tupelo seemed to Alice full of hairy-cheeked swollen dead men and their wives. She cut out. She liked to watch the horses over here, and she rode them. A woman with a horse under her has a liquid thrill. Sex becomes the very thing she breathes. No mere husband can bring it to her. Sex is a gas from nature itself, and it is something muscular and prancing. It is not the disclosed little member under fat and fur.

Not having that, she chose nothing.

For years and years. She went out with the state senator, but he was just another ignorant blowhard.

She wanted somebody lean and famous to live with. Fat reaches the mind, she said, and goes in there so deep and so dull. She had a prejudice against fat people and fat children. She found herself being unkind to fat children. Fat to her meant a doomed complacency; she could not bear, offended to the bone, any more of it.

She taught her classes. Nobody works harder than a good high school teacher, and the work with the children was fine. She could see improvements every day. She won Teacher of the Year two years running. She went to the football games. She was at some of the basketball games, and everyone whispered, There she goes, Alice Lipsey, Alice Lipsey. She liked to turn off the television and read whatever some friend had told her was the Most Important Book in the World. Sometimes it was the Bible. Sometimes it was *Lady Chatterley's Lover*. She read them. She hungered, she thirsted, and she writhed.

Then came Ronnie Foot, who came to her. Had adored her and came to her door, which was by now the door of a nice little house with ivy on it. Alice had been to Europe and in other states, where she collected pieces from the eighteenth century, except for the ashtrays. She smoked Marlboros and did not care where she put the ashes. She had a Harley Davidson ashtray, an Amnesty International ashtray, an ACLU ashtray, and she had been soberly to their conventions. Sometimes she liked to crank up the old Harley and ride it out in the weeds, as she told me eventually. She went at night and by stealth, with no helmet, avoiding the local goons, to whom a prize like this on a Harley was a major bust. A woman on a motorcycle with no helmet, hair streaming, excites a Mississippi cop, with his recent greasy supper in him, to no end. Nobody hates people having a good time more than a town cop in north Mississippi.

He had seen her, with her hair in the wind, driving by his big house. She barely knew he existed. But he came to her door in one of his modest rock and roll suits, knocking politely at 9:30 P.M. He had a rhythm in his knock. She'd never heard a rhythm like that. It occurred again: *knock knock de . . . knock knock.*

He was out there in a blue outfit with just some rhinestones in the lapels, and nowhere else.

He came in the house. Alice is a pretty and very short little woman. Her hair has turned gray at the temples, just a little bit. I say pretty, but what is that? I never went for Alice myself, she had narrow eyes and a severe look from her; you could take the beams from her eyes, fold them, and have something in your wallet that would light up the next night experience you had. She had merciless bright eyes.

Out at the big house. Big rich millionaire's
house. Alice looks all through it. It looks like a
resort hotel in Florida, except not as clean and
almost everything has been broken. All the
modern fixtures have been rammed against and
snapped, broken. The odor of dead and shitty
chickens somehow reaches in, caresses the
nose. These people have laid down a founda-
tion of bad-smelling broken things, and she
knows it instantly. You go upstairs where there
is an aquarium full of everything you can fish
for in Mississippi. The aquarium takes up a
twenty-by-twenty tank and otherwise you stand
on a bright emerald rug, looking at it. There is
an acned man in a white sea hat named Captain
Facks and you think he might be a nephew or
another broken-down has-been from a better
job, only he seems to love it so much, explain-
ing about all the fish in the rivers and the lakes
and the ponds of Mississippi; you get intrigued
by the lecture. There is a big gar in there and
a monstrous catfish, and large bass, both small-
mouth and largemouth. Everything, Captain
Facks explains, would each of them eat each
other, except we have balanced the aquarium

so that everything is big and it can fight. She looked around and saw some five- and six-pound bream swimming around. Nothing in here can eat itself because all the members, our citizens of the deep, he proclaimed, can afford to, or need to, eat each other. This is a perfect world in the world of $H_2O$, he said.

Then, after they'd seen that world, Ronnie Foot took her to another room, where there was simply a couch and fur things on the floor. She wanted to see the room where there were sea sounds, and then she saw the really old man on the bed. It was clean in there and it already looked like a funeral parlor. He refused to show her any more of the house.

She refused to continue the night.

He drove her back home. She had barely thought of making love with him. She went asleep instantly, in a hard black sleep going to soft, blacker and blacker, no dreams.

Then I myself came to her door. By now it was October, I believe, and we had great soothing orange moons hanging over the town. She did not strike me as one easily consumed. I told her how Jack was concerned. She told me how concerned she was about Jack's being concerned. It struck me then that concernedness was like a ball thrown back and forth among the three of us: light, easy to catch, very civil sport. She was struck by my concern and liked me for it, I must believe. She brought out her thighs and ate me twice. I'd barely seen her and, once dry, went back to Jack with a healthy report, though I must say I was still stunned by the voracious range of a woman who seemed made for light civility and patter. Say it again: the hungry dark beneath our bright and serene veneers can cause a man to reestimate the whole town. Why, she made sounds like a drowning woman, not an ounce of contrition, not an ounce of expectation beyond the event.

"She is in no way cheap or cheapened," I told Jack. "She's still a queen, your daughter. A very strong woman. I like her laugh. She could—I tell you—eat up all the tawdry measures of Foot without tasting a damned thing."

I was swearing away and Jack believed me. He liked the part when I bragged on his daughter for her discretion.

But my new wife-to-be was angry about my mood. How did she know?

She knew so thoroughly that she wouldn't iron or cook for me any more. She knew. I must be a blank sheet of paper on which is written *fornication.* I was some jerk in one of Nathaniel Hawthorne's tales.

"Say, dear, what could possibly be the matter?"

The heartfelt moans of hypocrisy shook me. What an inadvertent lecher I was, what a dog; I could not bear my transparency and my red lying face. I stood up in the air of the house, then went out standing in the air of the town. Good oxygen fled from me with a sort of hideous laughter, it seemed; I could not breathe the kind air I used to breathe. I felt to be a new alien to my town, and my sin ran around my legs like a dog dyed red.

I had allegiance to Jack, I had allegiance to my wife-to-be, who sat staring forward with hurt on her brow. I never blurted out a thing, could not destroy a dear heart with something stupidly truthful, and then anyway why did she pretend to know? What about her petulance? What about invasion of privacy? This nation was founded on principles of life, liberty, the pursuit of happiness, and no invasion of privacy. Eh? *Eh?*

"You seem so chilly and aloof," I said. Hadn't I fought for American things in Korea? Hadn't I kept my body pure in my first marriage, long ago?

With Alice the schoolteacher, didn't I want some more? Wasn't there—yes, there was—a thing so deeply random, out of all sequence in our naked collision, a brilliant hunger like the hunger of the coyote nation around my shoulders? The sense of it almost petrified me, and I know I was a man without his natural rhythm because of it, dragged through the day like a zombie with his head smoldering, walking falsely; lying down and sleeping falsely, as my woman would not touch me, a creature breathing gas from a tormenting new world. An infant could have read the signs.

I wanted to play some tennis and she wouldn't play with me. We had a fight. I accused her of hysterical malice. I drank more, smoked twice as many Luckies. Then I charged away in my little old Renault, two rackets by me, a new can of balls, swearing at her I'd play somebody, then, I wasn't going to stay around the old cabin and catch *her* damned fever, that was for goddamned true! I can growl a good *God damn* with the best of Southern rednecks. Get a Southern man mad, pollute our place with her little weirdness, would she? Well. Yeah. Better believe it.

I got to the university courts, watched the coeds batting and rallying. In my college days they cared less about the sport. Nowadays, there are little women who can trim your ass out there. I was watching how well the coeds played when she turned up herself, all rigged out in shorts and tennis shoes, and sat right beside me: Alice Lipsey. How did *she* know I'd be here? What is this sense they have? What is this canniness? Her sudden presence lit up the air around us and I was afraid.

"Who did you come with?" I asked her.

I was a little ashamed of my white thighs and calves. She was tanned and looked good in the leg, a good sixteen years younger, as she was. I was shaking, unnerved. A minute ago I had been a mere humble observer of the coeds, these children. Now I was in the world of our (yes, mine too) hunger, with the air twice as thin. There is a line of wonderful full green magnolia trees alongside the college courts. Plants of this size must produce a great amount of oxygen. But all my air was going into the smile of Alice; she was drinking my air. I have never seen a more magnificent woman than little Alice at that moment. Her perfect little butt was made for the shorts.

"Ronnie brought me. But I was hoping you'd be here. They say you're very good. It's a wonder we didn't meet before."

"Where's the rock star?"

"He's back in his Jaguar or his Porsche. Don't remember what he brought this time. He's pretending to listen to some cuts from his new album. The thing is, he's shy of universities. Even this one, which ain't your Harvard. He's got on his shorts and you ought to see his legs. Something magnificent, all his dancing on the stage. He told me he was afraid of being recognized and swarmed, but I tell you, he's simply afraid."

She was borne up by the love and attention she'd had lately, and you could tell it. The blossom was on her cheeks. Her racket was white, some new ceramic job by Wilson. I wondered if Foot was giving her any direct cash.

"He's losing his hair," she said. Then I noticed her hair, cut shorter and now blacker, as if to meet me and torment me. "I was going to teach him some, but then I saw you out here. I felt so evil. You looked so good."

We took a court. The girl had a great knowledge of herself and what she could do, and she almost beat me. I wouldn't let her. Thank God for the rules, where you get to rest and take water in odd games. I won the first set at 6–3 and thought, She's given up; but she's everywhere, running freely without ever having smoked a cigarette, and already, though I won, she was almost too much for me. I said, Say, baby, it's only a girl, and then I was behind 2–5 in the second set. My lungs were crying. In mid-October the air was thin and good, but Alice was simply outplaying me. I won a couple of more games by falling back and lobbing her; then she finished the set, with a little odd drop shot.

Ronnie Foot had come up without my notice and stood with his long body and white tennis cap against the fence, as if clawing to get to her, or me.

I never realized he was that tall or had such a scratchy speaking voice. He had a voice that reminded you of the bored little policemen who used to kill civil rights workers in the sixties. Then he could go into an alto range.

"Beat this ol' man ass and then we git outta here, beebie."

He never looked at me. I resented the fact she was even *close* to him.

So I got my wind and knocked off everything, imagining myself at twenty-five years of age. I was a dead man when it was finished. I was heaving and about to go into stroke. I have no idea what she said to me or what Foot did. I had beaten the girl who amazed me. Big deal.

She didn't like to lose either.

I saw the dark blue car go away, somewhere out there beyond the green rustling hands of the magnolias, go away into their calamity, go away, darling stupid things, into that death we all saw.

I had a presentiment at the time. I had no gun, so I went by Jack's café to get his .38 pistol. Anthony was there, the black man who runs the café in Jack's absence, and I fibbed and told him, if he would, to go in the back and call Jack. Jack had a phone there. Jack hated to use the phone and hated anybody who called him; he could not remember when any good news ever came over the phone. In the meantime I put the .38 in my tennis bag. I was out like a ghost, trespassing in all dimensions.

I drove up to the Foot mansion, full of wrath. Gunfire was already coming out of the place before I got there. I made a mistake and drove up near the chickens. The .22 bullets were skidding around. I came at the exact hour when Gramps was at it. I am a creature of fortune. Things were skinning the car. The bullets hit around the hubcaps of the Renault and one bullet hit my bag, as I set it down and removed the .38. I had enlarged dreams, seeing the blue-black car sitting out front of the mansion. While I was ducking I identified Gramps's window. I saw him up there, blazing away with his little automatic: *pip pip pip de pip pip*. Chickens jumped in my car and the dust scooted up.

God and man, how lonely I was out there, and such an interloper, such an annoying prophet! It was Chosin Reservoir reduced to the basic ingredients, man shooting at what was not himself. You cannot imagine how almost crazy I went with the .38 in my hand. It seemed viciously heavy, trying to move upward on its own, and I was pulling it as down as I could. Down, sport, hey! Not again.

But alas I shot it once at the window with the skinny figure hanging out, banging toward me. *pip pip.* Let go one for Jack's wounded hand, for his daughter's catastrophe after commingling with me, wonderful me, Hey Jack! There must be some reward for me, consumed as I was. There can't be just a bad goodbye!

Gramps is up there blazing away. He thinks he sees something out there, something annoying on the edge of the house lights, something moving, something like—it must be—a bigger chicken, a rooster, yeah, we'll let him rest in peace. Rip him up, little bullets, rip him up!

Comes something greatly sinister into his life, something has shot at *him,* something loud and proud has whistled in from the chicken yard. Also, he can hear an even bigger silence from downstairs. People are rushing, some person has knocked over something, says his mind, melting his heart of stone, and then he goes out the window, almost all his old skinny body out the window, looking, sniffing, for what he now knows was a bullet.

No second occurrence comes. No, he is left there in the awful silence, when everybody else is going on to do things and he has nothing to do. He sees headlight beams on the ceiling, but he is helpless at catching them. In fact, he is just standing there, an old man holding his exhausted .22 automatic.

The rooms have waked up. There is a rushing sound. Gramps fears fire. Better anything than die in a hideous big fire.

Tell you, boys, I ain't . . . gets to do this . . . his underwear is off, he is naked, trying not to burn up. Runs out to the man in the deep green Renault. (There is hardly anything else to talk about except how a man transports himself in cars such as these or, the second subject, how a man lives, shooting deadly without wounding anything, shee-it, monsieurs.)

I was away before anybody came out of the house. But I drove out of the place, feeling much the coward, seeing that old man run out naked toward my car. He was the first out. I fled. Oh, children, I fled. Such uttermost the coward, the peacenik, the fiend has been offered and I run. I only suggested there should be a reply. Even at my age, I have no more control than a shy midget.

I went home and sat down. I had been fond of these evenings before. My lover came to me and knelt down, asking what she could do to console me. I felt I was in deep trouble, for having fired the shot and seeing the old man come out running naked toward me. It is curious that she was now so interested in my distress. There must have been something hideous in my eyes.

She removed my tennis shoes. She wanted me to have a shower and allow her to massage my back. I obliged her, still scared and reeling, loving the comforts of home, loving her hands on my back. My lover is a light and tender person. She has that blond hair charging from her scalp, an event like a horse race. She has the lovely feet, small and fine toes; she has the red dress, the titties, and everything a man needs in his bosom. She has the legs that reach, hoisting her along. She has the open full-lipped mouth that Marilyn Monroe had. Her whole mien, I've often thought, is that of a question ready to be answered immediately I could feel this even in her hands as she massaged me. I'd had nothing like this since Japan in R and R. I just lay there and accepted her ministrations.

Unless you're talking; then talk destroys. Your mouth emits things like a furnace. What you meant was already burnt up.

The awful thing I had seen was Alice's death, her ruin and then the graveyard. Jack was right and I knew it, and I was terribly, infinitely sad. I cannot account for pulling the trigger of the .38 except as a feeble curse at the future, a hollering against time itself.

Yet I woke in the morning with my head sour and full of scolding, a man too old to bear the wrath of his own pranks. I hadn't shot a gun in thirty-six years, and I could find nothing in the act except malicious nonsense. Every shred of valor had fled in my sleep, all the magic presentiment was gone. Cold sober daylight nagged and whined around my brain. I dreaded seeing anyone. But I'd have to return the gun to Jack.

"Why'd you need my piece?" asked Jack.

"Nothing. I went off my head. I just fired a round in disgust and here it is back. Here's fifty cents for the bullet."

"What a funny damned thing you've turned into."

"I was funny last night, all right."

"Where did the bullet go?"

"Say . . . it just went to hell."

"Real nice. Just give me a dollar even for the coffee and we've got it. But you're a funny damned thing."

I stop at the dead center of myself, knowing something is wrong in this hemisphere, and I am reaching toward it so as to wrest it out like a rotten plum in the syrup of some foul metaphor like that.

It is Alice and her dreadful destruction that
I am feeling, the presentiment comes back and
Jack can see something hideous in my eyes and
I know he can see it because my eyes hurt,
and his bright old eyes aimed at me hurt too.

"You are too quiet and short," he said.
"You scared hell out of my man Anthony last
night."

"I apologize, and I hope it's accepted."

"Were you drunk?"

"Not a bit. Maybe I should have been. I
shot at old Gramps Foot," I said. "He had his
twenty-two going already."

"Why?"

"Well, look at your hand. It's still there.
You say it means nothing but it's still there."

"So what?"

"It's still there, is what I'm saying."

"Do I look like a wise old man, so I can
finish all your thoughts for you? I have no idea
what you're thinking about."

Jack was standing there against the
counter, wearing a Hong Kong khaki shirt with
a maroon tie next to his throat. I looked at his
shoes. He was wearing tan ankle boots. Looking up, you saw the brown tweed trousers with
the white thread in them. I wondered if Jack
spent much time plotting to look this elegant.
I had never thought of this before, I had simply
assumed he *was* elegant, with no special

thought. I had come down here in my tossed-on black cotton pants and—what?—red-and-black flannel shirt.

At this time the tune "Suspicious Minds" came on the radio. I knew this version of the Elvis tune. It was done by the Fine Young Cannibals, which hearkens back. It had a nice hard drive to it, and the message increased in my mind. Alice is going to die and the date lies almost delicious in my mind, as if I'd bitten off a piece of the calendar. All the news of last night was true, and I was right, and I was not a fool.

"You are under the moon," said Jack.

He went back to freshen our coffee. He adds cinammon. Comes across your tongue with a sweet piquance.

"Nothing at all," I said.

The professor's daughter came to our house after we were married. My wife didn't know why she was here, and actually neither did I. She brought a gift, totally unnecessary, and she was looking very young but in Reebacks or however you spell it, these expensive tennis shoes. She had been an addict of pills and once had a

deeply negative attitude, but now she was working at Lakeside Hospital itself in Memphis, the
place where she was cured, as a counselor. She
seemed to have a gift for helping others. My
wife didn't know who she was or why she was
here. Neither did the professor's daughter. She
was a little puffed around the eyes, though sol-
idly beautiful and much shorter in her tennis
shoes. Her hair was long, black, and radiant
within itself. She was a little sunburned in the
wind in her convertible. She had no clear message except that I and Jack had seen her in the
car with Ronnie Foot and she wanted to make
the horrible explanation. She ate very little of
the lunch we had for her. I was eating plenty
and acting like food itself—usually a sort of
inconvenience to me—was my usual occupation. Yes, hell, we have all kinds of food in here
and I eat it, all day, and feel that good folks
should just lie around and stew in digestion,
never having an attitude. The preacher used to
come in for a big feed at my mother's house,
and all thought went instantly away except for
*mes compliments au chef,* etc., except for me, who
never ate that much when I was twelve, saying
in my mind, What a using beneficiary of my
parents' graces is the pastor, eh. I was hypocrit-
ing away during the lunch with this unravenous
beauty. *Fart,* eh, yes, well, much to be said on
both sides, *oooh, barp.* Getting horny as I ate,

too. Old minister wants back to his bedroom and makes up some spiritual laws about how this brunette should be sucking him, reaching further into second law of thermodynamics, the law of entropy, which means we all need our gravy, not just the usual enclosed world which is losing its sources day by day. But she wouldn't eat.

She was a friendly jolt from outside but my wife didn't like it, having considered me the friendly jolt for a long while and being very married just recently. An enormous thing will come into your new marriage and then the third law goes haywire, because there is no third law. I was much older, and she counted on me to not let any third laws pass without telling her. So I would say, Begone my secrets, my old fartness can have a sway just by its stubborn belligerence.

"I had to say hooray for the both of you and your marriage," the professor's daughter said. "I feel that you can't ever be anything unless you're married. Ronnie Foot said he wanted to marry me. That was the first thing he said."

"Eat me" was the second thing he said, I supposed. There is, I thought as I thought about Alice too, an enormous concubine in these slight women; the facts are startling, the wanting is an enormity.

"What do you think about your father now he is dead?" I blurted out callously. God knows why I said this except I wanted mightily to know.

She paused from not eating to light a long cigarette. I wondered whether therapy made everyone this jumpy and pleasant. Why was she even *here*? I wondered. What was she trying to redeem? It struck me then that she thought I was actually concerned about her, which I truly hadn't been. But the pathetic broke in on me and I was suddenly hers.

"I'm astounded that he *was* my father," she said. "Dad was such a snob, always pretending that modern life confused him."

"You aren't confused at all?" asked my wife.

"If I were married I think it would break down the little confusion that there is. I feel that people in general know a great deal more than they let on, and that , that it takes only the correct . . . prompting. . . . Like a garden, the seeds are already there. To me, it would be the right . . . marriage."

I saw my wife looking at me.

The professor's daughter went on.

"I liked speed because it made me live *every* fact. But I know now that it is madness to live every fact, taking away even the damage to the body and the mind."

"So?" I asked.

"It is better to be wrong in our old prejudices about love and marriage than to know everything. It's better to be wrong than to be a roving encyclopedia."

"Then . . .?" I went on.

"I'm ready to quit knowing and simply to be sane and live. I'm ready," she said.

When she left, my wife told me, "Say, I think she wants to be your second wife. She wants you to have the both of us."

I was flattered.

"Always nice to have a standby," I said. Fool.

The wife was not amused.

I was so old that one day I got scared and borrowed a friend's Harley. My friend, the sculptor Bill Beckwith, had a sublime 1950 panhead he'd rebuilt; had the old suicide shift bar on it. I struck out for the lower part of the state, my hair all fleecy in the helmet, the wind battering me like a cuff from an old friend. I did not know my destination; I only knew I was afraid of being old and I had to venture into something on this old elegant bright-brown motorcycle. My joints were unused to all the movements and I was hurting on the first night, which I spent in a beachside motel in Biloxi. My back was killing me. Behind me was an alarmed wife, but I could not help it, I had to be here, waking up in pain and staring at the brown water of the Mississippi Gulf. The Mississippi poured out and made the water dingy. You realized that the gulf here was the sewage of all middle America. It was not a bad place to be. You had the feeling of immense geographical significance.

I took off my boots and went wading in the water, pants rolled up like old Prufrock's on the beach. It was winter and I was an old man with white legs and feet, suffering the chilly water. I was no film star ageing gracefully and getting better-looking every day. I was the victim of age, age! I shouted at the dirty water, which rolled in sluggishly over my white calves. The gulls were feeding and lifting. I looked for the oldest of them. An old dingy one, please. Finally I saw him. He was getting all the fish. The old dingy one was getting all the fish! And he was so greedy; like an old retired bastard down in St. Petersburg, he was consuming everything around him, and the younger gulls were complaining.

I was inspired.

The soreness left my joints.

I hopped on the bike and went away on the way to Pensacola. I'd heard of a motorcycle club down there at Cack's, a bar. I headed there. Going through the Bankhead tunnel in Mobile, I heard myself, heard the sublime Har-

ley I was riding—1950, early Korea—dashed
back and forth on the walls as sound, the pro-
found roaring as if a rapid overamplified heart
were knocking at the tiles. I had then the might
I required in my tiny passage down the alley of
time. What a magnificent illusion! What a
splendid lie!

I went on to meet and drink with the bikers
at Cack's bar, wanting to know them, because a
part of me was kin to them. But I found them
dull and stupid. Rudeness as a way of life is as
dim as pleasantness, really. People who are
missing teeth and fingers for no goddamned
good reason aren't really that interesting as a
group. I don't think slaughtering the hell out of
the King's English every time one draws breath
obtains much, finally, either.

I heard one good comment from a lad in
his thirties, though. He had on his black Harley
tee shirt and was putting down the mug of his
thirtieth beer that day. He put his hand to his
eyes, rubbing out the hurtful crust.

"Christ, I remember when I was alive," he
said.

It was a comforting trip. The bikers wor-
shiped the '50 pan-head and insisted I spend
the night in a smelly house on a couch with the
body odor of a real heller who'd slept there a
month without bathing. Then I pushed on,
back to my clean home in the north of the state
of Mississippi.

Even when it rained on me on the highway, I never called myself an old fool, and I remembered the ancient sea gull.

I thought of Jack, who was even another generation older.

I thought of Alice and wondered who was eating her tonight, gave an idle but knowing guess.

Thought of my wife, with her blond hair charging and her sighs.

When I reached the lights of our little town, I was sorely missing my wife. My old man was a traveling salesman, and now I felt especially akin to him. Never understood it before. The town seemed to throb with improbable and deep life, beyond its tiny geometry.

I knew I was home.

I knew it was all the trip I needed to make, for a long while.

Have I forgotten to say that Jack's café is roofed with tin? The rain strikes it and you are held inside by a divine comfort, separated from the rain by a few mere feet. It drives into your young dreams, when the monsters were out but you were tucked away in the cave with your quilt and your thumb, their huge feeble claws three feet away and never any closer.

But when you are older, you are supposed to be wiser, and they will drag you in when they can.

We were out on the golf course and we were playing the eighth green. I was playing at golf, strolling along with Jack, being just a bit wiser at my strokes so I wouldn't embarrass him. The eighth green is where he was shot. But this afternoon the Foot mansion was quiet. I double-bogied the hole and wasn't let down. It was a tough one. Jack parred it but didn't seem to take much pleasure from it. I looked through the trees in the swamp and saw what he must have seen already. There was Alice's Mazda parked in the drive.

I pretended I hadn't seen it and faked being occupied with my new golf clubs. The clubs looked imposing, though golf remained unappetizing to me. As a game. I didn't like Nature hanging around everything, getting in your way. I guess the walking is good for you, a thing you must consider if you are old like me and Jack. My shoes were muddy from trying to find my ball. I would see my ball leap in the air and shout inwardly, Fool! Fool! Nature yanked my ball down into nasty and frustrating places.

"I've got an idea," said Jack.

"So?" I said.

"Don't we owe them something?" he said.

"What?"

"I knew I was going to do something. Look at the extra balls I've got in the bottom of my bag."

He pulled out his clubs and dumped over his bag. There must have been fifty golf balls in there. Now they were all over the green. He rounded them up with his putter and set a tee on the hump overlooking the swamp.

"There's nobody else here and all the time we need," he said.

He put all his clubs back in the bag, then teed up a ball. There was the swamp and the leafless trees and, rising, the Foot mansion on the other side.

"I bought her that little yellow car. Look where it brought her," he said.

Then he smacked into the ball with his eight-iron. The ball rose beautifully over the swamp. I could not see it going down, but then I heard a loud *whap!* as it hit the house itself. He proceeded to put ball after ball on the tee and send them lifting in the same beautiful measured stroke, so that I could imagine a rain of balls knocking against the monstrous house and could see them bouncing, smacking and curling, and even smashing the windows.

It was growing dark when he finished.

"I guess they know who it's from," said

Jack, flushed and done. "I guess they will know."

I couldn't get over the quietness over there.

So the wife and I were getting to need a classier house and we rented one out in the country, a nice old mansion that dated from 1870 or so, two miles from town. Two enormous magnolias in front and a turnaround drive and a Porsche in front of it. We had dogs and four cats. We had propane gas. We had 120 acres with a pond. We had deer lice and ticks on the dogs. We had the best music from enormous speakers from three stereo units. We were working on the old wood of the house, bringing it back to its prime. Theater people had lived in here and painted the floors black. Deer and rabbits were all over the place, and I slept with the coyotes around my head. It took five hours to mow the lawn.

    I mowed the lawn and put a badminton set

up. We got sweaty playing badminton. I got ready for a game every day. We were having a ball every day. My old man was a traveling salesman. I asked him wasn't it boring and depressing? and he said, No, son, I had a ball every day. That seemed to me a reasonable way to go about it. I put a croquet court up. I put stakes up for horseshoes. She could hurl those horseshoes better than reason. She knew the game, the high toss and the way she made it scramble toward the post—what a wrist on her! She never gave up. She never cut me any slack. Played with her head down and very meditative. It is a sweet thing to see a woman go after things, seizing the day.

She went around half naked in shorts and a bound-up tee shirt. It was certainly nice to be married, having all the nooky and the smiles. Suck nip.

I was doing the lawn late one Saturday evening, working a square under the pecan trees, sincerely as a lashed dog, it must have seemed to her, for I saw the ghost of Alice on the fence, practically lying on the top rail, her dress thrown out over the white poles. She was in the shadows but very authentic. Because it really *was* Alice, not her phantom.

"What the hell are you doing?" she asked. I looked down the hill at the street and there was a lean red Jaguar convertible. Nobody else was to be seen. "I'm by myself," she said, after I'd cut the mower. There I was, oily with sweat, grass bits clinging to my bare legs, a happy freak of the suburbs.

"Mister husband." She giggled. "Both you and the old man are nuts, true nuts. I can't even talk to him about that golf ball adventure. Called him up and scolded him, but he just listened, said thank you, and hung up. He won't talk to me. I'm going to make one of you talk, though."

"You're high as a kite on something or you wouldn't even be here," I said.

"Nobody can see me from here. Haven't I found the place? Just perfect. And maybe finally found the right drug. The invisible-maker. I'm in a movie, honey. Only you can't see me. What a state. You have any idea how long this old forty-one-year-old woman has waited for something like this?"

"With Foot, though. With Foot and his millions I even think the money stinks. What he sings . . . so labored, loud . . . and shallow!" I cried out. "His money, his foul Foot millions."

"Oh, shut up. Maybe I never had a chance to be shallow before. Want to know what he says when he's in that certain mood?"

"What mood?"

"You were in the mood one night with me. You ought to know. But you were extremely civilized. Know what?" She started giggling.

" 'Gimme some hole,' he says. He's such a rough awful customer! 'Gimme some hole, 'Lice.' "

I suppose I was looking horrified.

"So I want to be shallow. What did the liberal arts ever get me? I also"—she drew her hand around as in a ghost ballet, getting a silly *Gone With the Wind* voice into it—"want to be admired from afahhhr."

Then she went away, saying, "Nothing can stop me now. We sat there and saw those golf balls bouncing in the yard, hitting the windows. Why, we just laughed. We thought they'd never stop. Old Gramps thought it was some eggs come back for revenge."

Then she was gone in the silky motor sound of the Jaguar.

We had an odd August wind blowing around, no hint of rain, just a vicious hot blow roaming. Large hot quietness going everywhere for no reason, the devil's wind out there smarting off at the tiny citizens; take that, all you insects and chaff, *whiff, whiff*.

I saw Ed Morgan and wanted a tall television antenna from his appliance store. The black guy who came out was a mean man, chomping a cigar. I'd never seen a mean-talking black man like this. He said he wanted $100 to put up the TV antenna and wanted compensation for his trip out here. I thought his price was steep. Also, I didn't like his attitude or his snarling punching eyes. Who did he take me for, a white idiot?

"I'll put up the antenna myself. Don't bully me," I said.

"How 'bout fifty?"

"How 'bout thirty?"

He'd made me angry and I became a hard dealer.

There was a very slow lean old black man with him. They worked awhile outdoors. I wasn't paying much attention, me in my big house, white man with considerable dollars in the bank, my wife going around half naked, nooky, terribly clever to be this way. Suck nip.

Then the lean black was out there alone. I overheard the mean black guy talking to him, telling him to just hold the wire and he'd be back. I looked out and the old lean man was holding a slack guide wire from the antenna pole. He was in our dog yard holding a slack wire, and he stood there for a whole hour, shifting around but still holding the wire.

I thought of being a big conversational man and telling him it was useless, come in for a drink of water. But in his old eyes there was a duty and he did it. He stood there holding the slack wire, beyond reason and hope.

I was glad I wasn't him. I would not want to be pitied that way. He had on pathetic old darkie overalls. He was standing in the hot sun.

His face was made out of a certain wondering that gathered the wrinkles to his eyes.

He just stood there, impossible.

Finally he was a statue dedicated to stupid labor, bees nesting in his ears.

I began hollering at my wife for her shortcomings. She left the house, 11 P.M. I'd quit drinking and smoking. She brought me back a bottle of rye and a pack of Luckies, too. I hadn't smoked for two weeks. I must have been a horrible nuisance.

I took a drink and a smoke.

Then I was normal. My lungs and my liver cried out: At last, again! The old abuse! I am a confessed major organ beater. I should turn myself in on the hotline to normalcy.

We went to Shiloh to see the rushing loud old ghosts. Heard the deafening silent volleys in the orchard. Went humbly into the souvenir and history place, saw the movie with the startling lecture about the numbers killed. Nothing really registered that much with me; I did not care if this was the first "modern battle." I will not bleed any more with the solemn historians, making their living by their accountants' blood and their thin armchair poetry about the "horrible misunderstanding." I have written about almost everything else but my war, and I think it's best I keep it that way.

I was a simple young distraught fool in Korea—an armed one, very nervous, very quick on the trigger; had the firepower of two dozen wretched Confederates. If only I would quit hiding and point the right way. A couple of times I did, and for that I got the Silver Star.

So we were watching the light rain come down on the helpless and cynical fields of nature, sighing back to us in their great yawn: hickory trees, oaks, ash, maple, pine—blood dripping through all of them out of the flat dry autumn leaves, practically shrieking here and there in the maples. There's not a damned thing to say except Shiloh happened, a great standoff pointing ahead to the fields of Flanders with Brit and Hun slaughtering each other's poets.

Because I was so preoccupied, I had two wrecks driving the Porsche, almost. The Porsche was a bit too fancy for me, really. I belonged more to the old putting Renault, which gasped around like the dutiful lung of a bard on two packs of Pall Malls. Despite my bad driving, my wife lay over and hugged me, then took me in her mouth.

I was feeling for the old dead sad Confederates and Yankees. Out of the swift thousands killed, how many of them had anything like a Porsche ride and a bit of mouth from the little woman?

A wise guy once told me things were always better and worse than you imagined them. They were at least in heaven, which no doubt makes a mouth job look like snot from another world, some loogie with wings on it.

I became angrier and angrier. My wife could barely see me. She was alarmed. I was alarmed, and I was sick of being a mere husband, standing and waiting for tragedy, scribbling my notes—just sitting there in my suits in the morning, collecting money and giving them something. Business had never been better. My marriage had increased my credence. People could not keep from giving me money, and they had their cousins and in-laws come in.

Making money was so easy and I hated it.

I was so rich I felt like a scoundrel.

I wanted to drive somewhere very badly, and so this time it had to be Nashville. I'd never been to Music City, U.S.A. Also I wanted a new pair of rough-out boots. The Porsche made you want to go everywhere. My wife wanted to go too. You get up in those big cuts of rock and slide down into the city with your Porsche hugging the lane in the big rain, eighteen-wheelers trying to bury you and get to their ugly women so as to get on the home hayride, darlin', nothing like it. I met one of their women at a Waffle Hut near the Ramada where we checked in. Ignorant, proud, full of gossip, and covered with bad sallow skin. Looked to be about a terribly old nineteen. You had to plead for ice water, etc. Two bearded punks were baiting her. She hardly had the time, y'all, to get around. There is a truckline conspiracy with its own music, claiming that trucking is an interesting way of life. I have never seen in all my years a beautiful trucker's woman. Them big rigs keep on comin', bro, huge, hoggish, dangerous, full of zero music, just a sort of spiteful poetry about those not stupid enough to climb into one of them. I must've been low to write down these thoughts. The Grand Old Opry—I wanted to go and love everybody. Another plastic ripoff costing $12 per ticket and a parking lot the size of a major university. Not a voice in the whole crowd, and the poor sidemen kicking it along, bored as truck drivers. I skipped the boots. Came on back home. You get a place like Nashville that tries to mass-produce heart and soul, and what's really there is a sad nineteen-year-old working the Waffle Hut counter, looking out at no prospect at all.

But I met a fellow at an Exxon station who belies all the last paragraph. He was the mechanic that came right over to the Ramada when I needed him. My battery was dead and he came over in the rain. He was cheerful and expert, even loving the rain, in his great yellow slickers and boots. You could tell he loved his work, getting cars going, nothing to it. It was raining like hell, like little cold pieces of hell. He went after the job and was a little disappointed that I was right, the car only needed a good battery charge. He had good skin and marvelously dirty fingernails. Got us over at the station to check all the electricity on the car; exonerated the alternator. We went into a Denny's and had some coffee, waited on by two sallow Mormon-looking hags. Maybe it's the restaurant business that sucks life away. Bless them, they were friendly, but so sapped and bleak. Went back to the Exxon station and the swarming traffic of Trinity Lane. All ready. I thanked him. Pal in a storm. We fired back home, our little hugging bug among the rude trucks, angry about the ugly wives.

Nick, nick. Always at his fingernails. Has his fingernails at each other through most of the day. What can I do to fill myself up? What is this great space in me?

Gramps isn't doing too well. Daddy and Mama aren't too keen in the health realm. In fact, all of them have been in bad health for centuries. A thought will come over all that sidemeat and carbohydrates and hit and cause veritable flames. A thought runs down the old head and on out there to where there's a tiny fire on the ends of the feet and hands.

Snicks his fingernails.

Mama and Gramps dwell on things, give out snoutish noises: Bring on reality, Lord, let us reduce it to its greasy parts. They still kill their own chickens, buy their own oil, and put it into their giant new automobile—anything to get dirty. My God, they miss the filth of the other place. It's difficult to prove anything with clean hands.

Isn't there something to tear apart or wad together? We need some dumplings and mashed 'taters, Mama. Need 'em bad. Need to cook something with a grinning dim-eyed head on it, smiling like: Yes, eat me. I be a smile in your belly soon.

Everybody is fatter except for Daddy and Ronnie. They got the nervous energy, they got the get up and go, they got shotgun eyes. They got the long lope and the twist, leaning off from you, not even seeing anything close to them.

Love on further into the dark, where people squirm and make hard greasy choices. Look on into the multitude and settle on one or two they can rule, find somebody who will finally say, What a piece of work you are.

And Daddy, who never had the guts.

And Ronnie, who did.

Both of them well hung, both of them wild with willful ignorance. Both of them crazy with ownership. Gimme that. Want to hold something in my hand and reduce it to its greasy parts.

Ronnie gave Daddy a gold-plated Monopoly set last Christmas. People were flown into Memphis airport to play with Daddy while Ronnie was off at concerts. Though they are almost identically alike, Ronnie is embarrassed by his father in public. He is certain that he is at a station stratospherically beyond his father. For one thing, he now has bought and owns his own father, a dream hardly ever accomplished by your normal boy. Daddy is rough, he is fine.

Daddy is hell at Monopoly. He is rough at

it. The pieces are dinked and flaked off. The game is played with real ones, fives, tens, fifties, and hundreds. He is the leading Monopoly player in America, Daddy is. He takes showers and changes into different high-priced jogging suits while other people are stalling around thinking about the score.

Ronnie owns Mama and Gramps and Double Gramps too. He barely gives Double Gramps a thought, just pays and pays for his room, his being; gives a quick flash on the idea of Double Gramps every now and then, especially when he's in an airplane and the airplane is in the clouds.

That's when he expects to see the spirit of Double Gramps, a tiny gray clod of spirit making a hole in the clouds as it rushes like a turd to the right boot of God.

When *will* Double Gramps ever pass away? he wondered.

There is the name of a famous violinist that is so humorous to him that he uses it as a curse, an invocation of everything silly and prissy. It is the name *Yehudi Menuhin.* It breaks the band up. He will just sit there with his earphones on in the studio, and when there is a minor hitch in the recording, which he approaches impatiently and without rehearsal (yes, once the wiser member of the band told a reporter, "We consider playing in tune a purely European concept"), he says through his nose, "Yehudi Menuhin."

All the boys break up.

Sometimes he says to women he doesn't understand, "Yehudi Menuhin."

When anything breaks or is unsuccessful, he says, "Yehudi Menuhin."

It's a gas.

He retreats into the "vast carelessness" that Fitzgerald describes. Even before he was rich he had a vast carelessness. Carefulness is chicken and peas. Carefulness is nothing. He had a dollar for almost every chicken devoured by all the fools in Mississippi every month. The week was a long single day to Ronnie. He wore no watch. The week was one long day in odd installments. There was no purpose in the sun's rising except to bless him with more sycophants.

There was an eternity of gratitude owed him for picking up little Alice, a nobody schoolteacher from his hometown, six years older than he. He respected his hometown and its culture, be it ever so humble. It made a hell of a story. It made a hell of a tune.

He'd already written tunes to Alice.

That means he sat down and made three chords and made up some rhyming trifle. By the time the band took it over and made it thunderous beyond hearing, with Ronnie screaming on his knees, the tune was unrecognizable except as a howling at his own cock, which he owned. It was called "Don't Ever Say Goodbye When I Thought Your Name Was Hello."

Jack liked to wipe the glasses personally with a dish towel, as you see an old barkeep do in the movies. He hired no help except the cook and big Anthony, the black man who handled everything when Jack wanted some time away. Jack made the glasses look like gems. He wouldn't put up with any plastic or Styrofoam ware. His prices were lower than anybody's. His place was spotlessly clean. Have I forgotten to say that it was crowded late at night, when nothing else was open?

He had one black cook, a man who was versatile and hardly ever seen. Some nights they offered gumbo, some nights sausage, cheese, and pepperoni slices. There was the one thing on the board, and you ate either that or nothing. Or the pastries—cheesecake or hot fudge pie. The college students were wild for Jack's place. They adored Jack and his Hong Kong shirts, his proper carriage, his beaming spectacles, his Teddy Roosevelt hair, all white d slick.

Who could not love him, as old and elegant as he was? The image of benign rectitude, yet something loose and giving in his rare full smiles. The main issue was: Troublest not thyself. I am old and lean and handsome and I have known these things, little citizen.

In a way, that was the whole trouble. The old benign rectitude came back. The pillar of the community returned.

When I finally talked to him, almost a month since I'd seen him last, he did not want to look me in the eye. He was shading his eyes away from me and made great motions as he waited on the students.

The fact was he was terribly ashamed of the afternoon with the golf balls. I tried to joke about it, but I knew instantly he did not want it mentioned again.

"Jack, Jack. Are you there?"

"I'm here."

"I've talked to your daughter about that afternoon with the golf."

"So it happened."

"I'm not trying to joke about it."

"I believe the child has written me off as a fool. That makes us equal. There are other things to talk about. Let's talk about Korea, let's say pleasant things about your marriage. You've done awfully well!"

"I have a feeling, Jack," I began.

"Yes. We all will have a feeling."

He looked at me meaningfully.

I was thinking how terrible it was for Jack and me both never to get out of our heads again, neither drunk by liquor nor drunk with feeling. We were almost too old to be anything but wise now.

Several women, three or four, were in love with Jack. They were the ones who lingered with their coffee until one in the morning. Jack knew the widows and older divorcées in town better than anybody, though he never spoke a word about them and their secrets.

He was back into the Jack I first knew. He ventured into the shallow depths of feelings with his customers. And now he was a great football fan. He went to all the home games and had attitudes about plays. We had four fast black pass receivers and a fine young quarterback from Florida. Jack was a bit overzealous and full of math when our team won. He started talking more about the weather than he used to. In fact, he'd never ever mentioned weather before. We would play golf in the rain and he would never discuss it, just go ahead and hit through the inclemencies, while I hit another two-iron shot into the marsh. They say that only God can hit a one-iron, but I tried all of them. A set of clubs costs a lot, and you want to see how all of them can hit. Sometimes one will act like a miracle, and the ball will rise ahead in a perfect arc as intended.

The truth remains that I have never witnessed as masterful an act as old Jack delivering the eight-iron shots to the Foots' house.

It was a great shame to me to hear him talking now as if he hadn't meant it.

He had made me into an inferior being. There was a certain loss of friendship. He did not ask me to play golf with him. He was ashamed of his foolish passion, whereas I wanted to talk about how perfect it was. The other fact was that Alice wanted to talk to him too. He kept hanging up on her. His old pride would never admit that he had chipped that many golf balls at the mansion.

I can imagine her laughing and saying, "Hey, Pop!"

She called him Pop and she wanted to tell him that she was safe, quite all right. She's quit her job at the school.

The professor's daughter—*Delia,* wouldn't you know—comes around a cold block of Memphis in the snow. She's been kicked out of the counseling field because she's back on the stuff again. She is so dry her snatch is about to crawl inside her, looking for water. Exercise, exercise, she says to her poor long body and skinn legs. You can run anything else but the main pain out. You can never run the main pain out, never. Delia, Delia—didn't I once know somebody by that name? she asks. She can't go home because she can't face the mail. All of it's got a voice in it, all those envelopes are shouting at me: You owe and you are too late and now big ugly men are coming to your door, drag you out where you will be attacked by lawyers, led by Judas Iscariot, who is now head of the Highway Patrol; they will come in and look at what a dirty apartment you keep, and there are big pink, green, and blue stains on the walls everywhere to show every fault, every shadow of a bad thought or intention you ever had. You say you've got only three Quaaludes and five Ritalins left, all your contacts are busted, 'cause when you get to a phone you have all the quarters in the world, but the main pain cuts in, like the big pain, the cold slice of wind asking, Who is my daddy? Who was my daddy? Who am I? Was I talking to myself? I never used to talk to myself in the Used-To. I have all the quarters and I can't make a call.

That Ronnie Foot. I wanted so much, he promised so much.

I deserved all that, I guess. But he was the last straw, he and his limousine at Daddy's funeral. I was making some complaint one afternoon, and he got the chauffeur out, that yesy who's some nephew of the family, and

Ronnie took me back to the cemetery where he'd looked me up. I believe it was the first time I ever complained about anything. Who wants to complain to her groom when any day you could get married? He was such a fine man when he lay down naked beside me in that antique bed he had at the big house. I was amazed he drank nothing, smoked nothing, barely touched the dish of cocaine. It was I who was the hog on the cocaine. I couldn't get enough. I had it all ways. He was getting it into my sex by mashing huge amounts in. Then he took two sniffs himself and began coming all over me all night. I thought it was the honeymoon. I still have a vision of his tattoo on his chest racing back and forth above me. Most men with tattoos have pictures of other things and symbols on them. On his hairless muscular bulging chest was a perfect tattoo of *him*. His face had been done perfectly by some artist in Rangoon or somewhere. All is hazy and oriental.

But I made the complaint, maybe I had a headache or something, and he sat with me in the back of the limousine and kicked me out into the cemetery. About nine at night. And when he kicked me out—I mean used his foot and propelled my stoned fanny out just about graveside to Daddy, as he'd found me—he saw me on the grass and he said, "Yehudi Menuhin."

Then they drove off.

I was in my high heels and naked. At least it was dark. I had no keys. I had no personality. Even my car was lost; could not remember. It seemed years ago. I ran through some back yards and some woods and then I was there and broke in my old little perch. All the food was gone in the fridge, and the water had been turned off by the city. I fell asleep trying to chew an old apple.

But now, God damn it, I'm back, if I can get a Ritalin out of my purse. I am trying not to remember how I drank from the water left in the commode.

It was then, by a vast coincidence, I met Delia in an alley near the Rendezvous, a famous Memphis rib house. She was stumbling as I came out wiping the sauce off my lips with a handkerchief. A big snow had come in, and I was stranded at the Peabody, the plush hotel in Memphis where the ducks walk into the pond with music. It's a very nice hotel, and I didn't mind missing the flight to Dallas, a city that I loathe. I had never been snowed in before, and I wasn't exhilarated about talking at the small business convention I'd been invited to. The

SBC. I'd made the news in the national magazine. It was good to be on the loose in this odd weather. The snow was solid as iron under me. Then I got a whiff of garlic from one of the exhaust vents coming out, and it was Chosin Reservoir for a little while, but I didn't go nuts. Maybe I was too chubby to go nuts any more. My marriage had annulled all the nervous spots, and new fat was bathing the jumpy ends of me.

Enough about me. I was another white-haired bore at the Peabody, thinking of writing at least a poem about the snow to take home to my wife, who was using plenty of Revlon Eternagem, a rich body moisturizer.

"My child!" I said to her in the alley.

Soon we were in the warm luxury of the hotel room. She was skinny and ravished around the eyes. She was as old as I was, worse. I mentioned ordering up some food and she practically shouted at me.

But by now she had quit shivering, with the bedspread around her. She went to her purse and got a Ritalin.

"Why don't we empty out your purse and see what we are working with?" I said.

I took two of the Ritalins and pretty soon started blabbing away myself. There is pleasure in talk when you take this drug. Later I heard it described as a constant orgasm. It is used to regulate autistic children. Everything feels good. I must have talked for five hours. She would talk, then I would talk.

"Gimme another one of those!"

I took the pill and increased my monologue. Also, I wanted to move, race, shout, pursue the grail in the Dark Ages and slay any amount of Saracens, other sand niggers. I had the answer for the problem of Turkey. I had met the mean Turkish infantrymen in Korea, young men begging to crawl across rocks in the night and throttle a gook with wire. Food was sent up. Delia and I ate all the food. She jumped out of her poor old street-soiled dress and went at the curtains, ripping them down. Now she was dressed like a violent queen skeleton of the Nile, dying and mysterious. Her body was so thin I cannot even recall the impression of it as she transferred herself to the curtains.

Then we got in a violent argument, I can't remember what about, and I took her downstairs and kicked her out in the snow.

After that weekend I got terribly drunk one Friday afternoon. I drank a couple of bottles and went through the house yelling about the shortcomings of everything. Blacks live in filth, use food stamps, and make a hero out of Michael Jackson, a hideous plastic doll with a sissy voice. Little Michael buys a face like a white man's and now he and Paul McCartney, who hasn't been shit for fifteen years, push their millions around. Frank Sinatra is allowed to live, reeking of filth and thuggery. Friend of the President. Everybody vile is writing a book. I am writing a book. Do you wonder why the U.S.A. has no respect? Etc.

I woke up on the couch on Sunday morning and a war movie was going on TBS. My nerves were so gone, I could not stand it. I could not stand stupid large invasions and men being shot. I asked my wife please to turn it off. When I was better Monday morning, I saw the same movie sober and was absolutely complacent about it. So it happened. I felt ridiculous for all my bad attitudes. I wanted to apologize to Sinatra and Michael for my bad thoughts. They were probably good guys. I tendere apologies.

It's shitty to come out of a drunk so m and feeble. You even start thinking cops damn about you.

Went down to see Hooray Bugger, the old Delta blues men, they said. Mayb to the scene too late. He wore a Stetson h played horrible guitar, singing when he v to, and changed chords when he wanted to. Maybe he deserved it, he was so old and the last and so on. White people were everywhere with their cameras, hoping he would die on the spot. That's too cruel and wrong. No black people were in attendance.

Maybe, I was thinking, at the end, when I am the last Korean veteran alive, they will give me plenty of Ritalin and I will shout out my stories—covered with liver spots, a few sprigs of white hair on my head. Fifty cents a ticket, bring in your supper, drinks, coolers, everything.

Now lads and lasses, this is how it happened:

Ignorance ran like a wind, smelling of garlic and hot machine-gun bullets. The ejected shells of howitzers went off and made the snow give way. All of the squad had gathered into the black circle, rubbing their hands against the warm shells, ducking and rubbing. Until I got sick of it and said charge. Surprised the Chinese. Surprised myself. I was firing two carbines, one in each hand. Then I fell down when I was hit in the knee. But I'd frightened away their whole front line.

She kept her apartment. She liked to sleep there, being a woman of scandal. She did not care for the drugs any more. There was really only the main drug, cocaine, and otherwise there was only aspirin. She had eaten almost nothing but cantaloupes and oysters for the last three weeks, and she had been to the ruins of Yucatan with Foot. "Hey, Baby, I guess we all got to fall down sometime."

She wasn't going to put up with too much more from Foot.

She was on his regimen now. She had given up everything that would decrease her energy: red meat, eggs, chocolate, the rare cigarette. Potatoes, gravy, fried things. She had quit the school and she was a woman of scandal. The red Jaguar was parked out front and she had twenty thousand in cash in her purse on the floor. She was thin, tight, and breasty. He was out of town, playing in Denver, and her nipples were still sore from Foot's mouth. They had made love countless times, and it was always the same but in different places. They had slept in Jackie Collins's house in Los Angeles but the odor of raw sewage increased so much when she opened her mouth that their lovemaking and their sleep were disturbed, even getting to Foot. Even the Foot mansion, when everything was cooking and the old people were making around with their farts and apologetic snorts, was better than this. It was rumored that Sinatra wanted to meet

Foot, but they hung around Las Vegas and he never showed up, so Ronnie said they were canceling this engagement and they'd flown out, meeting the mere Burt Reynolds and then, for no reason, Conway Twitty. Alice held some sway after that and they flew to Asheville, where they visited the tomb of Thomas Wolfe; thence back to this town, while Foot said "Yehudi Menuhin!" fifty to seventy times. They encountered the grave of William Faulkner. Ronnie lay down on the concrete box and began making hunching motions on it, never giving up the night until he came, with a shout.

That was enough for Alice for a while. She made her way back to her house to sleep alone.

There was a call from Ronnie.

"Seen nothing yet," he said. "What else can they show me?"

Her sleep was bitten by great desperate nightmares.

Then for some reason she got on the phone to me.

My wife didn't like it. We had a thirty-minute fight about my concern for Alice and what kind of concern it was. I fought back and started igniting one Lucky after another. You say, you say, you say this, baby, I say that.

Concerning Ronnie Foot, I say there is a rule that nice guys finish last. Which should not give a leg up to every asshole, either.

You get over these constant storms and learn to be married all over again, every day.

But you must get off to the pond where the big bass are, down there. You must get to it at the wrong season, when nobody goes fishing. When it is cold and there is no fishing at all. Yes, me; it was me at the wrong time and I was by myself at a pond south of the city where a friend of mine caught an eight-pound bass during the last of that hot summer. I was there by myself, throwing out with an old spinning rod and loving the new cold water in the pond. It started to snow and I loved that too, because I had my wool overcoat on, the long nice wool-weave thing my wife gave me at Christmas. I threw out a few times and there was nothing going on. I threw and threw, switching lures from the hard plugs to the jointed wigglers. There must be something out there. I was moving up and down the dam in my new business-man's overcoat. Just on the chance of you women being out there. Because they told me once that all the really big-ass bass that hit are female. I was told to feel her and then knock her jaw off. I threw and threw, wanting to bring in a record bass for me, my wife. Just throw and throw, said my uncle, my namesake, and I had a weird little wobbling lure. I got one. I got a big bass and it wrapped itself around a tree limb deep in the water. I got off the boat with my tiny little embarrassed penis and got the fish, unwound the line, brought up the bass. My uncle was proud of me, my short bald uncle with no children who owned the plantation around us and shot a man when he was young because the man not only won the card game, he used a chair on my uncle's face. The judge let him walk free because the man he'd killed was from out of town. He was cheering with me now about the bass. Maybe he had no children but he was a hell of an uncle.

Back then around Lake, Mississippi, long long long ago.

I got nothing at the pond. I kept heaving into it, feeling like some kind of white man's illness around the ecology. Then I thought of the last thing. I'd go for the purple worm, that plastic thing in my tackle box. My tackle box looks like a tenement house on the East River in New York; there are so many tiers to understand, and I have about three ingredients to understand: shelter, nookie, respect.

Big bass takes the worm. I'm not thinking of anything except packing up. I picked up my rod and a huge bass was on. The snow was coming down and it was unlikely, but the big bass was on. I kicked over my tackle box, trying to bring him in, and ran down the dam. Then he was off. I'd missed him, and the snow was coming down twice as hard.

I had that great tug and I missed him. I didn't even have a story to tell. And that's why I've told this one.

Shoot-down train huffing by the rotting depot. Floor of tile—butts, sweat. You can walk around in it, sigh, think of some broken-down palazzo. The old depot is exactly the size of your waiting. You can walk around in it, sigh, think of your flat love all over again. Jump on to New Orleans. Get farther than these old floor tiles in the station. Please, please, I'm going to be somebody.

I felt this as an unpublished person, without my wife, without any credit except my enormous money.

Rails click. Petulant children crawl out of nasty insincere wombs, flashes of families. I had had too many drinks. Went to New Orleans very off the limit with booze, my wife not around. Went to Mobile and embarrassed friends. Was driven back by Mike Florence.

All places circulate around your sun. I roam with a stable room.

I was so bad I bought tickets to Los Angeles, just for the plane ride there and back.

Arrive LAX drunk, sick, shooting filthy language. This place is crowded, everybody dressed like a star. Nigger with chaps on, ladies trot in porno sandals, rich leather bags around dairy breasts. Get a goal, get a goal. Thing that pulled me through Korea. Get a goal. Heavy into some solid arrow. Don't get into all eye contact with all prancing nookie. I figured I was so handsome and wise, everybody was looking at me. This was not true.

But I did have one conversation, with a divorcing stepfather.

"A few years ago I was given the free run of a house, pleasure with the woman of the house, a house on a shady oak street, big house, on the condition I could abide the grinding banality of her children, who sucked the heart out of a fine day as a matter of ritual. They drove off thought by exercise, eating, and pretending that they had friends. I could not, however, fulfill the contract."

I have tried to delay the news.

I have tried.

Foot got in a bad mood and killed her with Gramps's .22.

Jack was away for three weeks and then he was back.

Friendly, polishing his glasses, human. Straight. He looked at me friendly, and the next day we played golf on a wet course.

The next day, without a note, he shot himself in the head with his pistol.

And all my wife and I have to say is Hey, Jack.

You must never believe Jack would kill himself, and in fact he did not, though his poor daughter died.

That it weren't true, but is, it was.

I was numb and confused. I had only had a piece of her, all of it sparkling and famous, and now she was in the ground.

I worried that Jack would do what I have

written because he was so calm at the funeral. His other daughters were there, and one of his wives. My wife and I took food down to Jack's house, feeling a little ridiculous because we had fed at Jack's café so often. Put the fried chicken and the macaroni-and-cheese dish down on the big table. His quarters were small and neat, extremely neat. There was not much he needed. He was a reader but he did not like having stacks of books or cases of them around. He bought them, read them, and then gave them away to the less fortunate. He told me he had a fine memory and it made him feel heavy to look at a lot of books together. Jack was light on his feet, even at seventy-eight.

But I picked up a book about the Eighth Army in Korea, and I was proud of reading this without going nuts. It tells the story.

At the same time the 1st Marine Division was fighting its way down the MSR, another equally fierce and important battle was being waged seventy air miles southwest of the Chosin Reservoir. . . . There, beyond the great barrier mountains that divide North Korea, Eighth Army and the Chinese were again locked in battle. The two forces had first clashed in early November, but the enemy had broken off the engagement. The succeeding weeks had done nothing to lessen the differences in their combat personalities. When they met for the second time, they could not have been more dissimilar; one was 6,000 miles from home, the other in its own backyard; one was boisterous and issued daily communiqués to the world, the other was taciturn; one had armor, artillery, and air cover, the other had men—180,000 of them; one had trucks of every size and shape, the other carried only what a man could pack on his back; one competed with itself for road space, the other glided overland from valley to valley, hilltop to hilltop; one left a trail wherever it went, the other left no trail at all; one didn't know where the other was, the other did; one hadn't read the tragedy that would soon be enacted, the other had written it.

After the Chinese launched their first-phase offensive and stunned Eighth Army, they had retired behind a range of harsh, inhospitable mountains and not been seen in force again. The dilemma facing General MacArthur was clear: should he dig in or resume the march to the Yalu? If he advanced, he risked another enemy counterattack; if he remained where he was, north of P'yongyang, he surrendered whatever initiative he had to the Chinese, who could then dictate the time and place of their next offensive. True to form, MacArthur chose to attack. With X Corps ensconced on the Yalu, the war ends, bringing peace and unity to Korea; the curtain comes down, the UN Command takes its bow, and the spear carriers are sent home. It was a scenario MacArthur had seen played out before, and each time it had ended in victory. Why not this time, too?

Indeed. Now the old boring history prof stands up, shaking the flakes out of his scalp. *No, class.* A big clumsy pointer over the very spot I was in Korea, running like a dog, in the vile frozen holes and out of them. I was learning to shoot everywhere. All my weapons jammed one afternoon and I was just pulling the trigger on the air, Chinese all around me. At Alice's wake, forgive me, but I read further into the book and heard the despair of one sergeant:

> I well remember the agony of meeting each incoming little group of survivors and learning who wouldn't be coming back. Even now, it is extremely upsetting to me. I recall beating the frozen ground with a stick I'd used to walk with and wanting to cry for Rex Gunnell and not being able to. I remember Rex had only recently been married; he'd told me his wife had never even cooked a meal for them.

Then further to the comment of Corporal Dan Thomas: "They usually attacked well after dark, often between midnight and three in the morning."

With the quilted suits, the tennis shoes, the smell of garlic, and all the whistles and bugles.

I live to say this. Jack lives.

Alice doesn't.

Oh, Alice. Hubba hubba, girl. After making it back from the Chinese and with my Silver Star all dogged away behind me, after having that night of you, and then yourself, a ghost talking to me, and then the last phone call, and then you dead.

Killed by a simple stupid millionaire rock star.

I was pulling my trigger finger in the air again.

They were playing the William Tell Overture on the great stereophonic speakers.

Double Gramps had finally died.

It was a vague numb tired event for them, not much of a ceremony. But it saddened Ronnie. Alice went out to console him.

He put a coke bottle on her head and said he was going to shoot it off her head, like in the song.

During the trial he described it as more capital boredom than capital crime.

Did Ronnie.

Jack stood up in the courtroom and declared that if the court freed Ronnie, he would kill him himself. All law-abiding citizens were amazed.

He was restrained, and the courtroom was awed.

Two days later, Ronnie, who had finally looked Jack straight in the eye, hung himself in the cell where he was kept. He had written a song to Alice which he wanted delivered to Jack.

They told me the news and I went to find Jack. Anthony told me he was out on the golf course. He was at the third hole when I reached him. He was hitting a nice approach with the wind against him, blowing his old hair.

I touched him and gave him the sheet of notebook paper, folded up and addressed to him.

Jack took it. Suddenly he seemed old, and I began crying. He had never looked so old and handsome before. The wind kept at him. His hands seemed full of liver spots. His eyes dimmed. He was barely carrying his weight. I thought he was going to fall. But he didn't.

"They gave me and you a certain hell,

Homer," he said to me. "They made us know everything."

He balled up the piece of notebook paper and chipped it up high in the wind, so high it came back to us and landed behind.

"No mercy," he said.